JOHN HENRY

HAMMERIN' HERO

Graphic Spin is published by Stone Arch Books
A Capstone Imprint
151 Good Counsel Drive, P.O. Box 669
Mankato, Minnesota 56002
www.capstonepub.com

Library of Congress Cataloging-in-Publication Data

Peters, Stephanie True, 1965-
John Henry, hammerin' hero : the graphic novel / retold by Stephanie True Peters ;
illustrated by Nelson Evergreen.
      p. cm. -- (Graphic spin)
ISBN 978-1-4342-1898-8 (library binding) -- ISBN 978-1-4342-2265-7 (pbk.)
1. John Henry (Legendary character)--Legends. 2. Graphic novels. 2. John
Henry (Legendary character)--Legends. 3. African Americans--Folklore. 4. Folklore--United
States.ffl I. Evergreen, Nelson, 1971- ill. II. Title. III. Title: John Henry, hammering hero.
PZ7.7.P44Jo 2010
741.5'973--dc22
                                                        2009029956

Summary: John Henry was destined to become a steel-driving legend. As a young man, he
makes his mark on the American railroads. But one day, a salesman comes to the railroad
camp, claiming that his hammering machine is superior to any worker. John Henry steps up
to challenge the man's machine, hoping to save the jobs of thousands of railroad workers.

Art Directors: Bob Lentz and Kay Fraser
Graphic Designer: Hilary Wacholz
Production Specialist: Michelle Biedscheid

Printed in the United States of America
in Stevens Point, Wisconsin.
112011
006489R

JOHN HENRY

HAMMERIN' HERO

RETOLD BY
STEPHANIE TRUE PETERS

ILLUSTRATED BY
NELSON EVERGREEN

STONE ARCH BOOKS
a capstone imprint

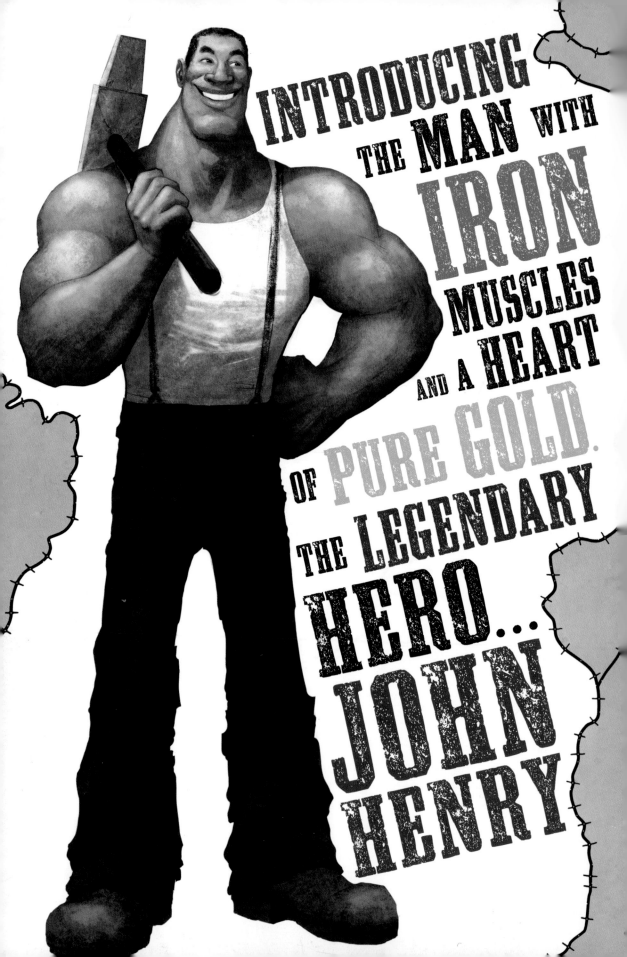

INTRODUCING THE MAN WITH IRON MUSCLES AND A HEART OF PURE GOLD. THE LEGENDARY HERO... JOHN HENRY

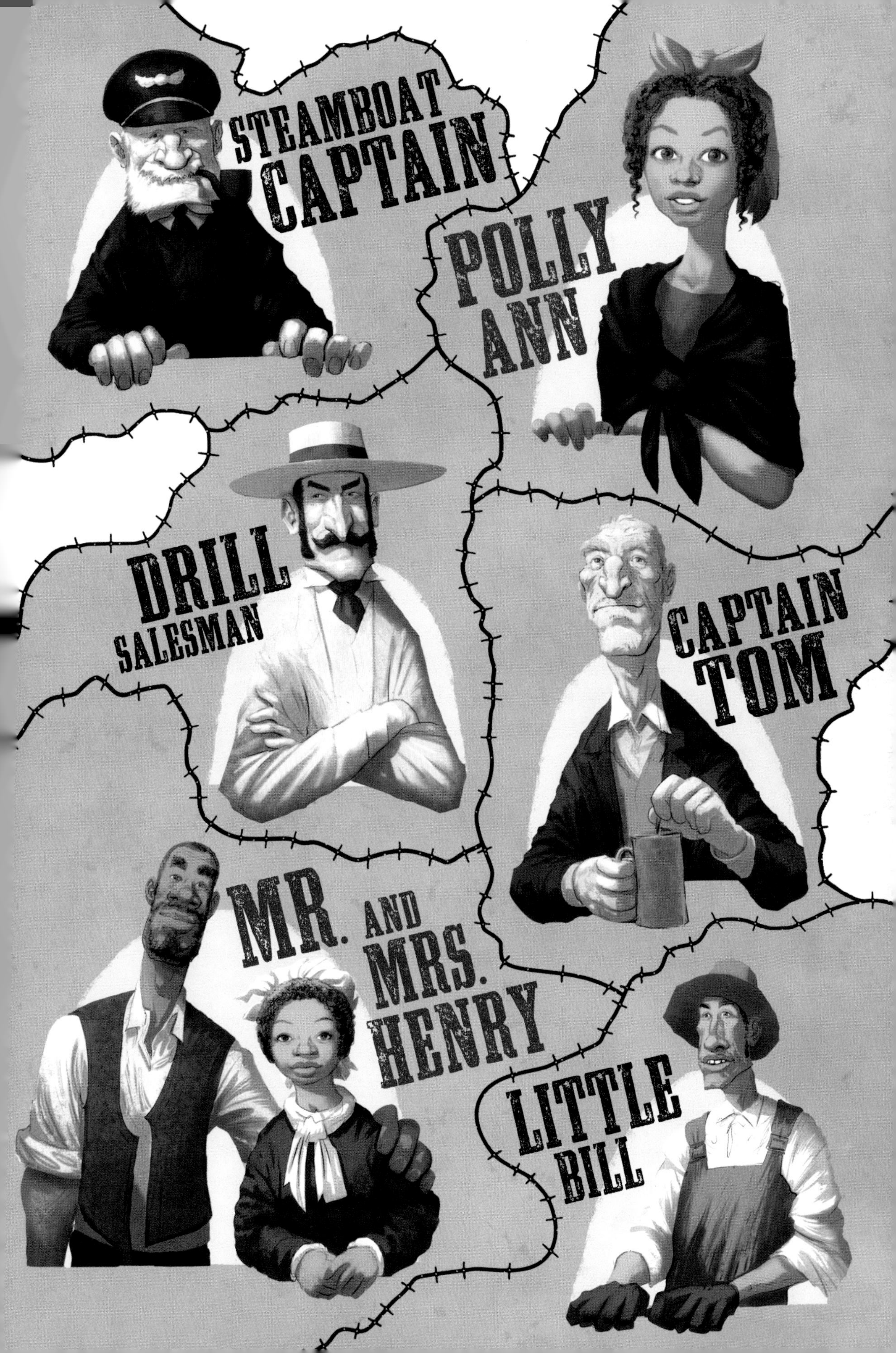
STEAMBOAT CAPTAIN
POLLY ANN
DRILL SALESMAN
CAPTAIN TOM
MR. AND MRS. HENRY
LITTLE BILL

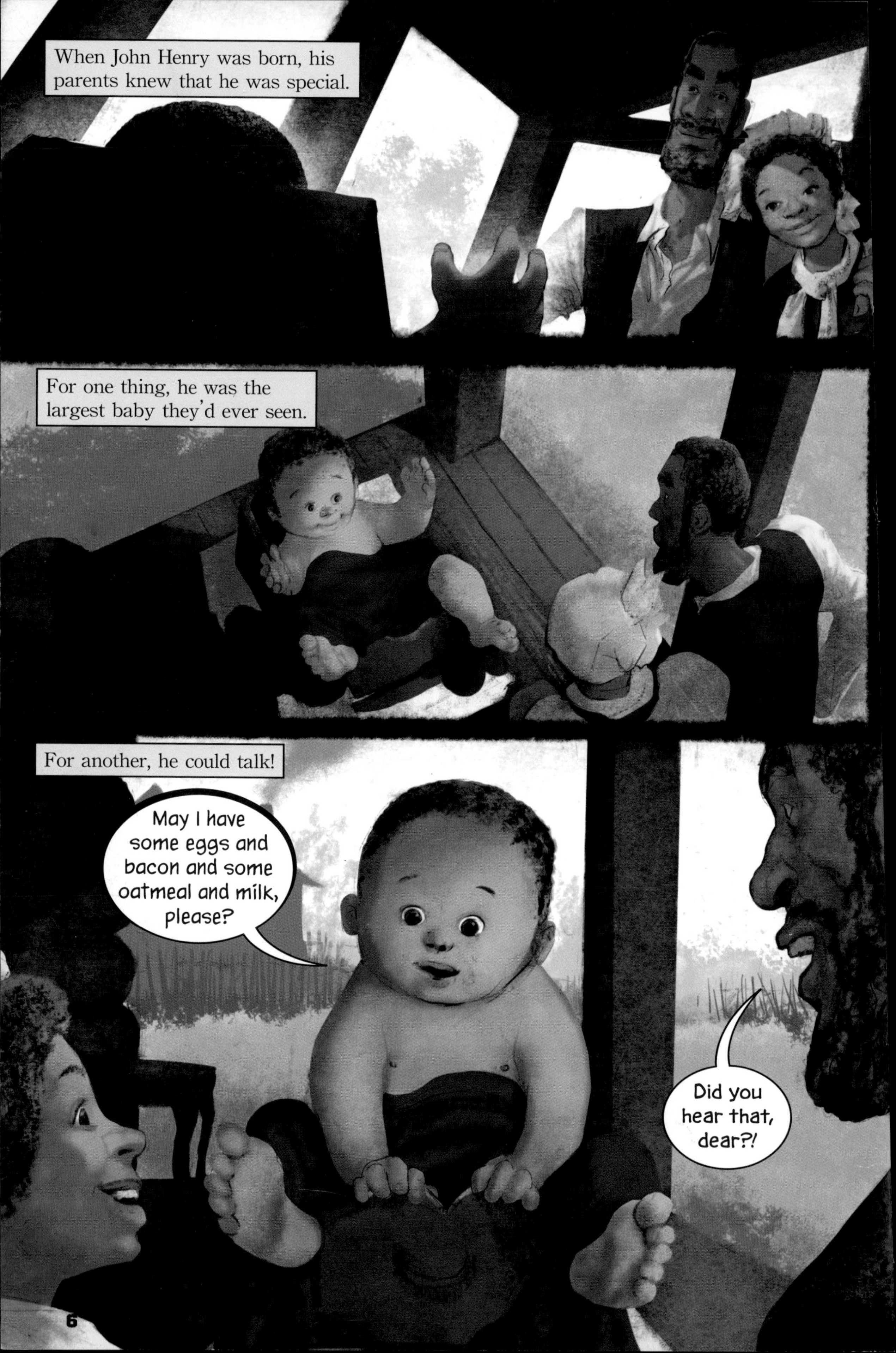

When John Henry was born, his parents knew that he was special.
For one thing, he was the largest baby they'd ever seen.
For another, he could talk!
May I have some eggs and bacon and some oatmeal and milk, please?
Did you hear that, dear?!

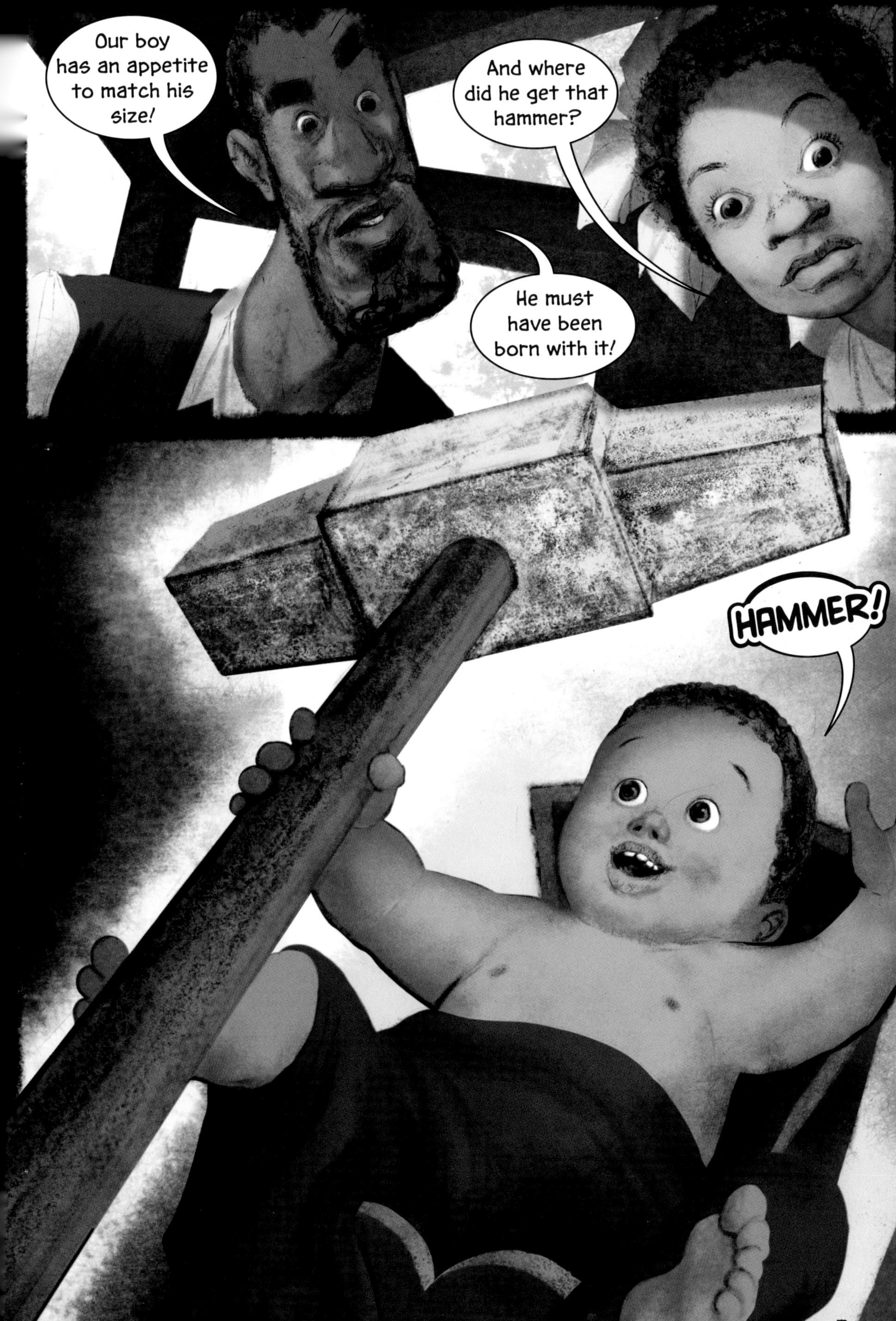
Our boy has an appetite to match his size!
And where did he get that hammer?
He must have been born with it!
HAMMER!

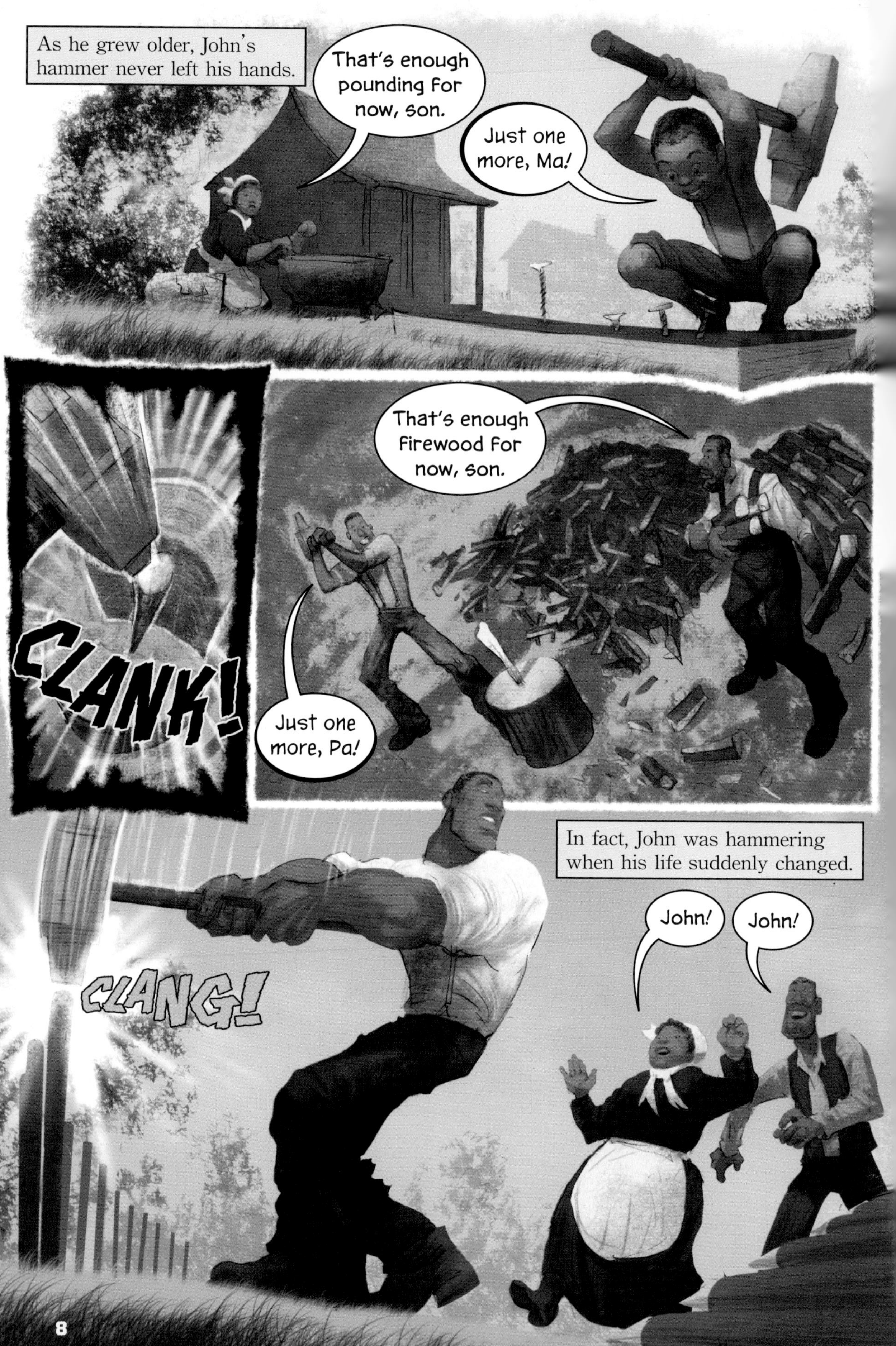

As he grew older, John's hammer never left his hands.
That's enough pounding for now, son.
Just one more, Ma!
CLANK!
That's enough firewood for now, son.
Just one more, Pa!
CLANG!
In fact, John was hammering when his life suddenly changed.
John!
John!

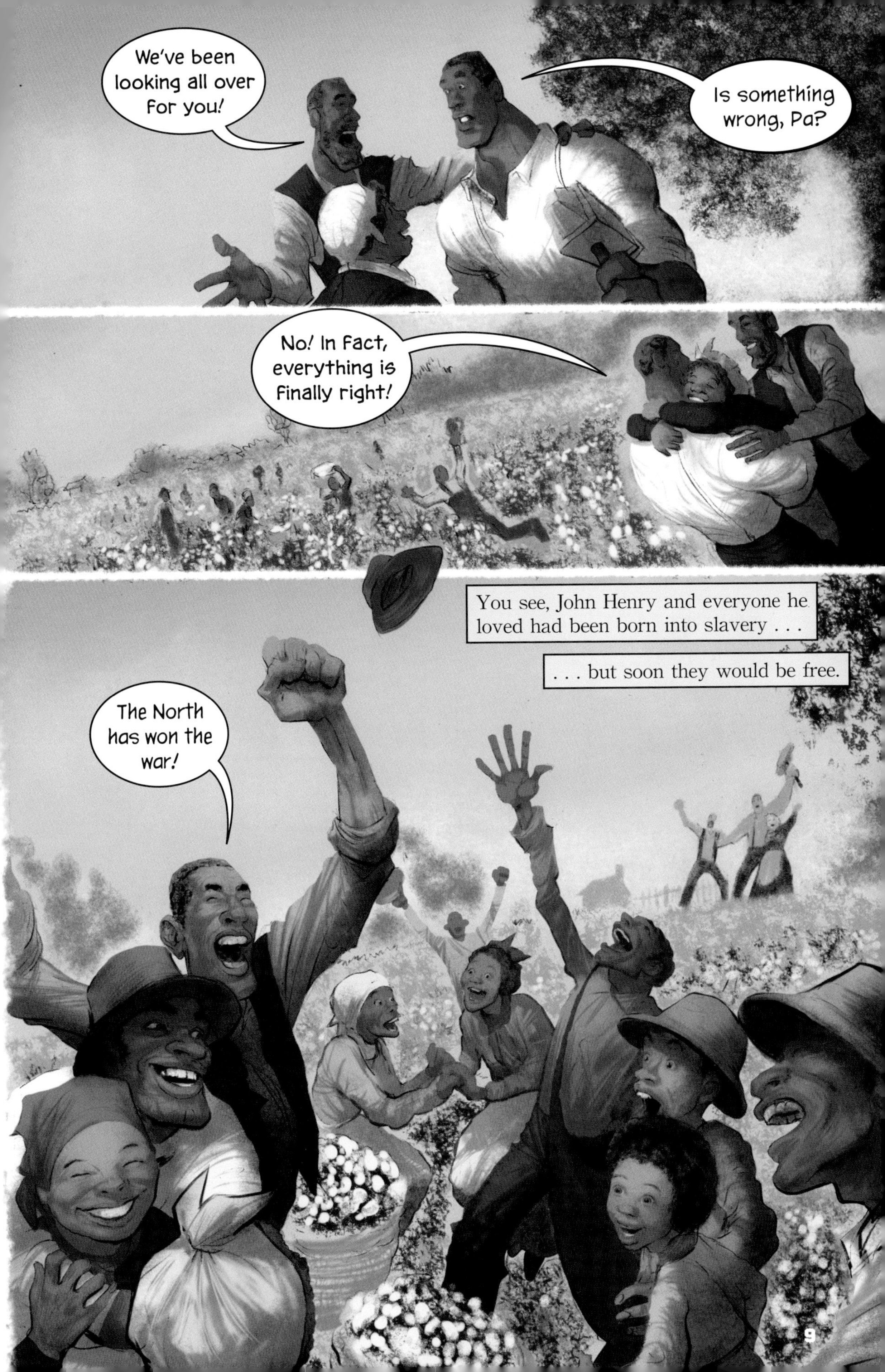
We've been looking all over for you!
Is something wrong, Pa?
No! In fact, everything is finally right!
You see, John Henry and everyone he loved had been born into slavery . . .
. . . but soon they would be free.
The North has won the war!

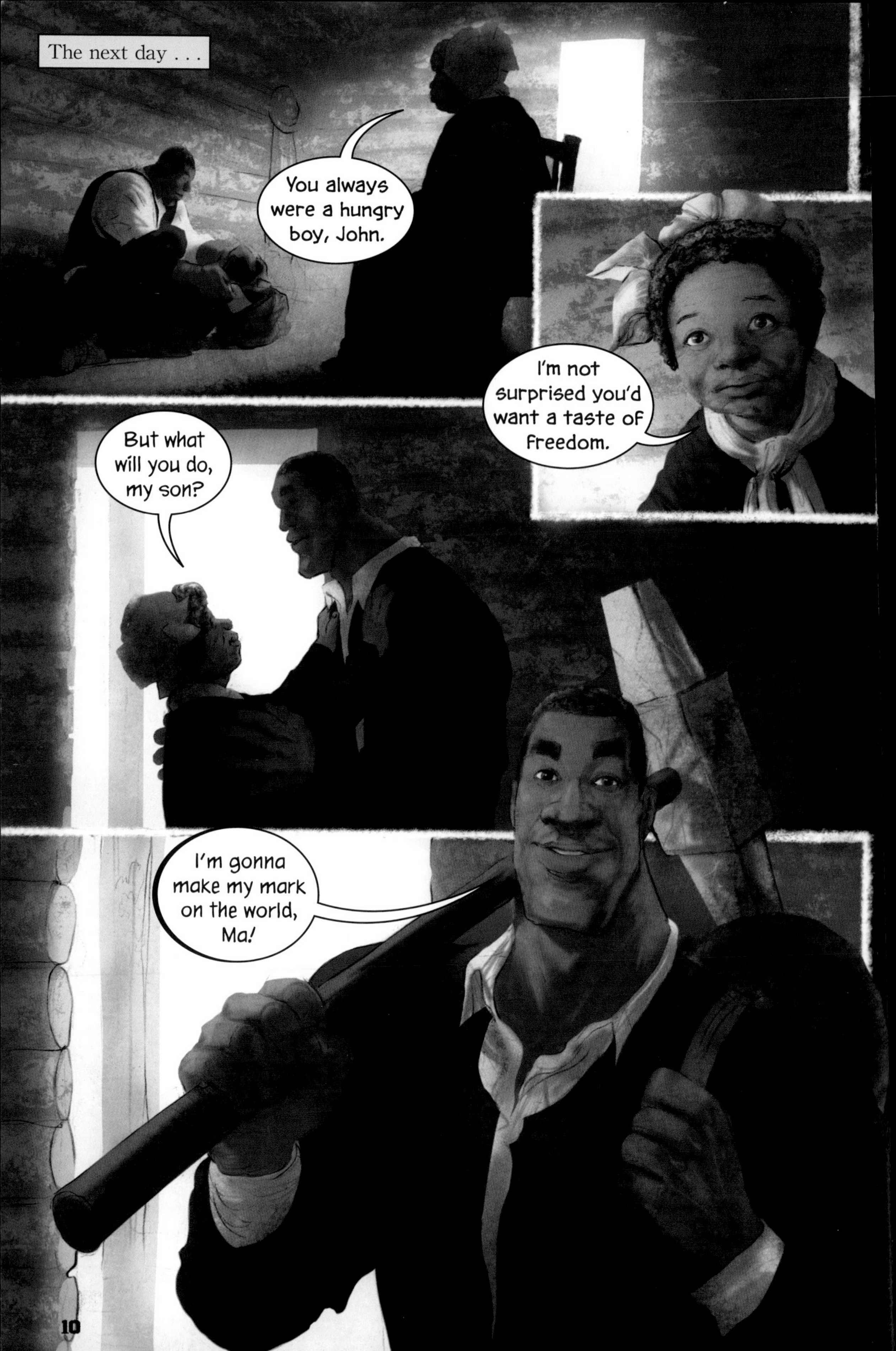

The next day . . .
You always were a hungry boy, John.
I'm not surprised you'd want a taste of freedom.
But what will you do, my son?
I'm gonna make my mark on the world, Ma!

That day, John set off, carrying his trusty hammer — and the weight of his family — on his shoulders.
Find your own path, son!
But never forget where you came from!

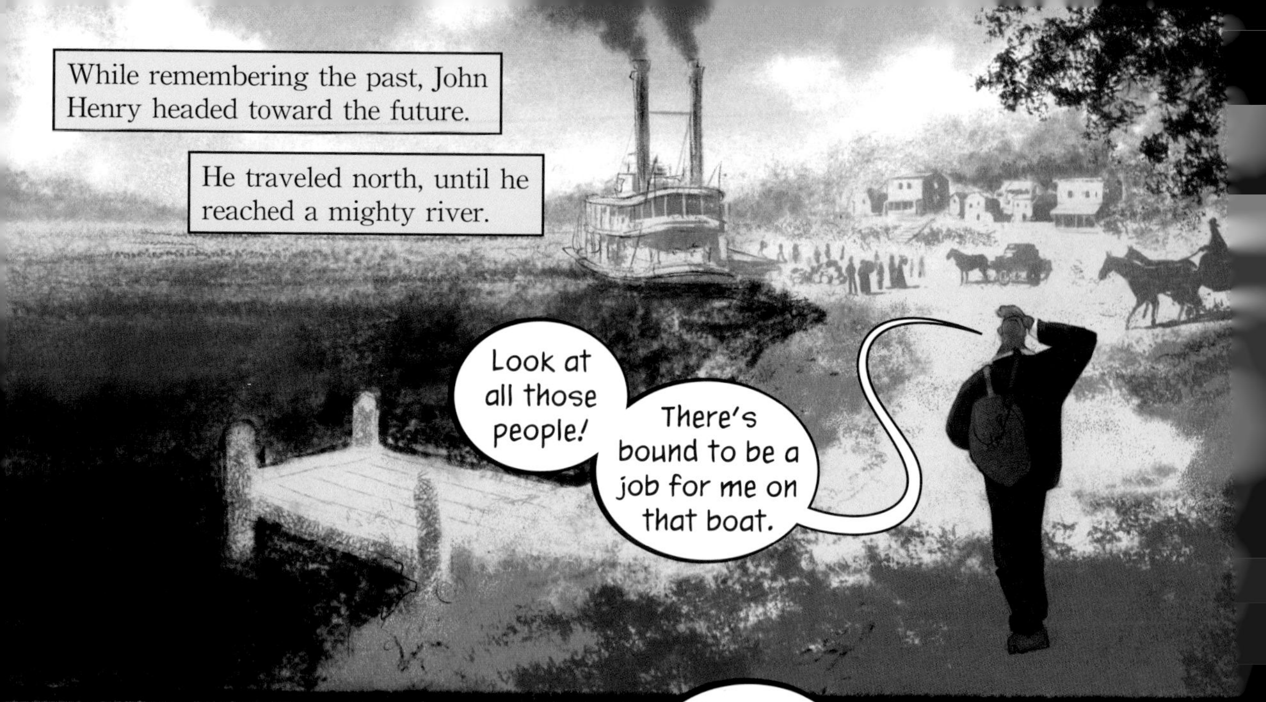
While remembering the past, John Henry headed toward the future.
He traveled north, until he reached a mighty river.
Look at all those people!
There's bound to be a job for me on that boat.

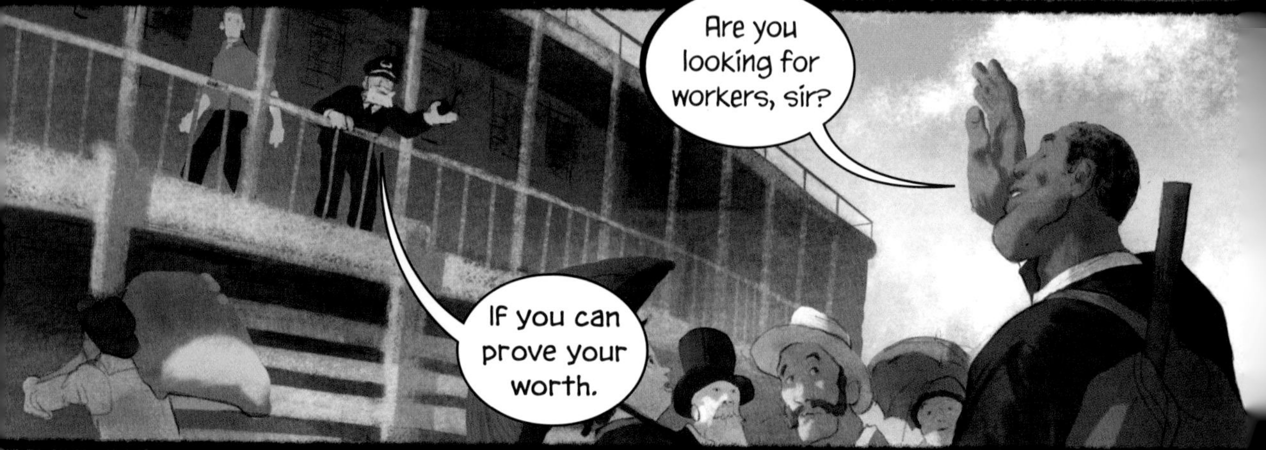
Are you looking for workers, sir?
If you can prove your worth.

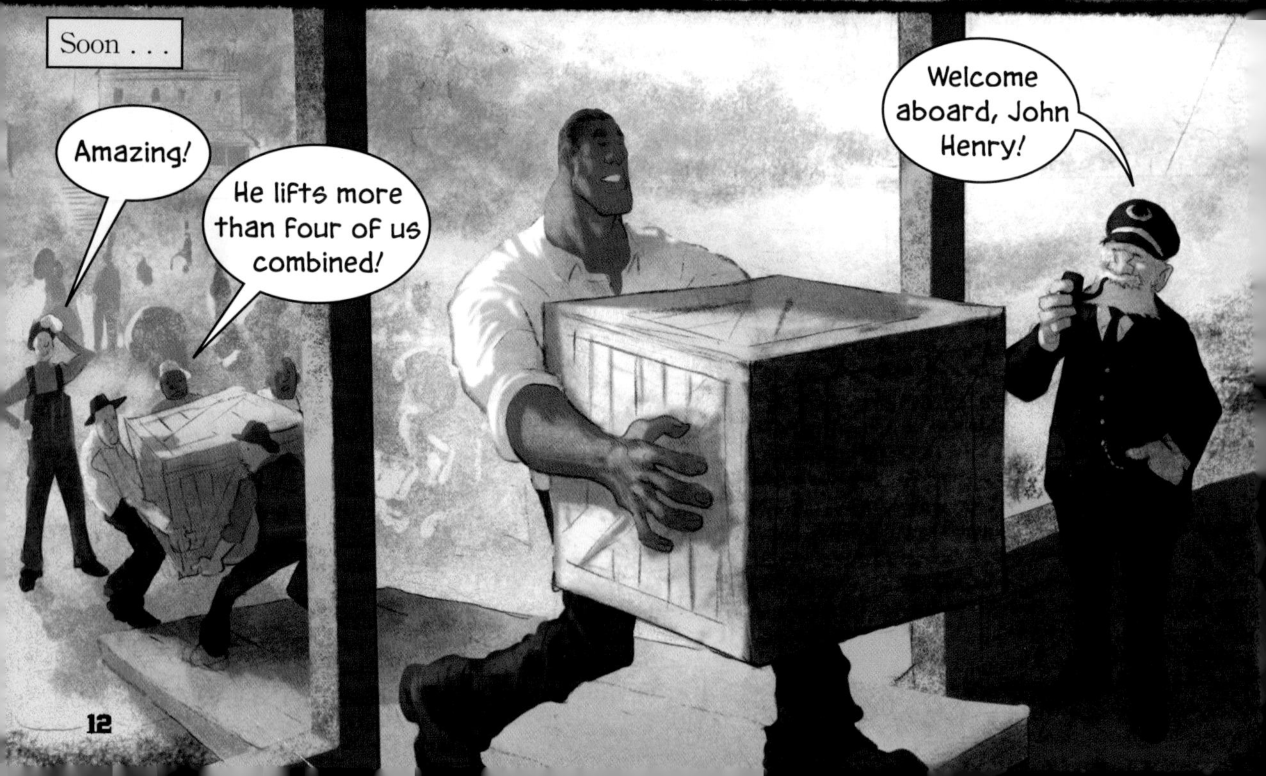
Soon . . .
Amazing!
He lifts more than four of us combined!
Welcome aboard, John Henry!

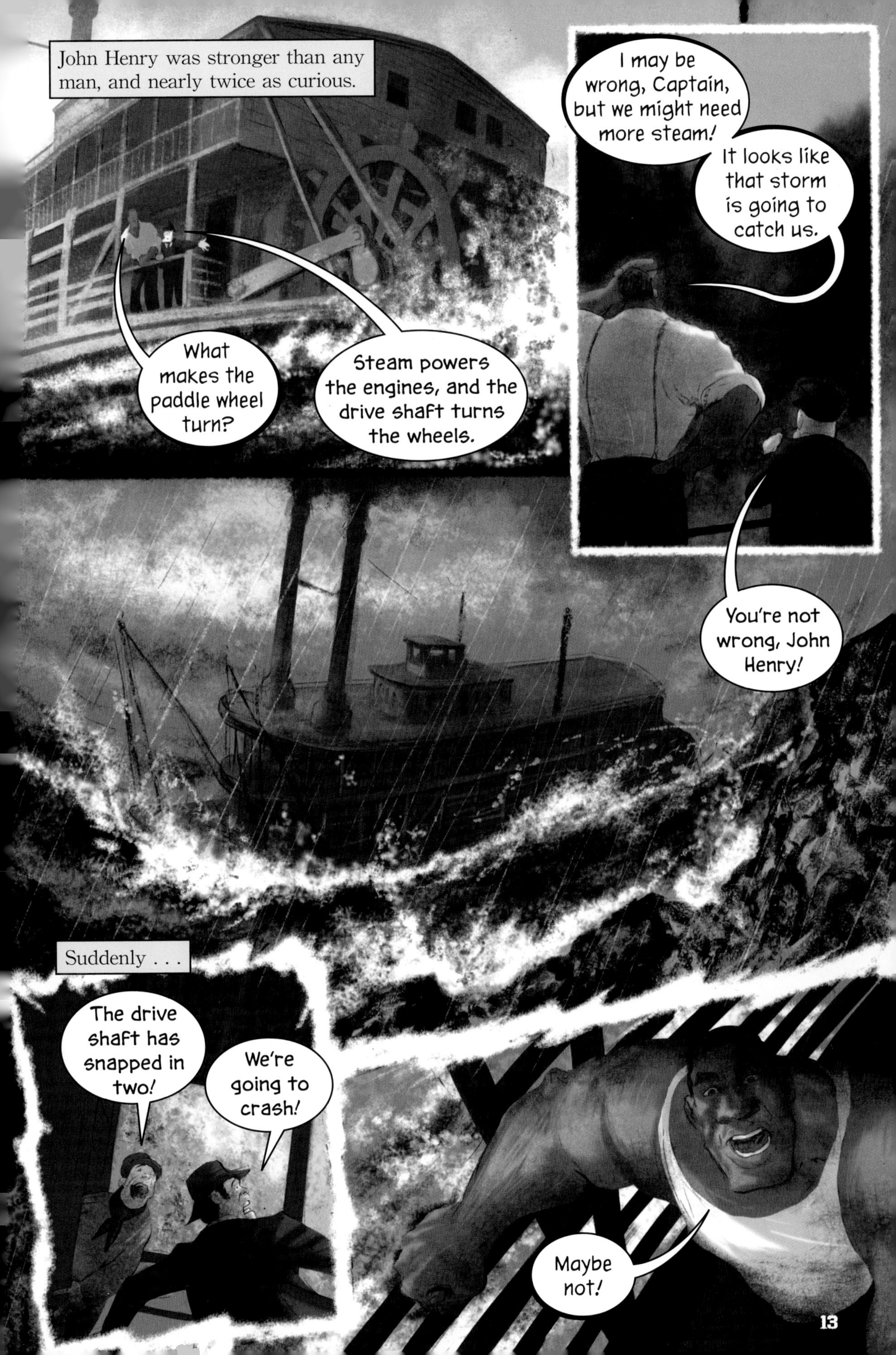
John Henry was stronger than any man, and nearly twice as curious.
What makes the paddle wheel turn?
Steam powers the engines, and the drive shaft turns the wheels.
I may be wrong, Captain, but we might need more steam!
It looks like that storm is going to catch us.
You're not wrong, John Henry!
Suddenly . . .
The drive shaft has snapped in two!
We're going to crash!
Maybe not!

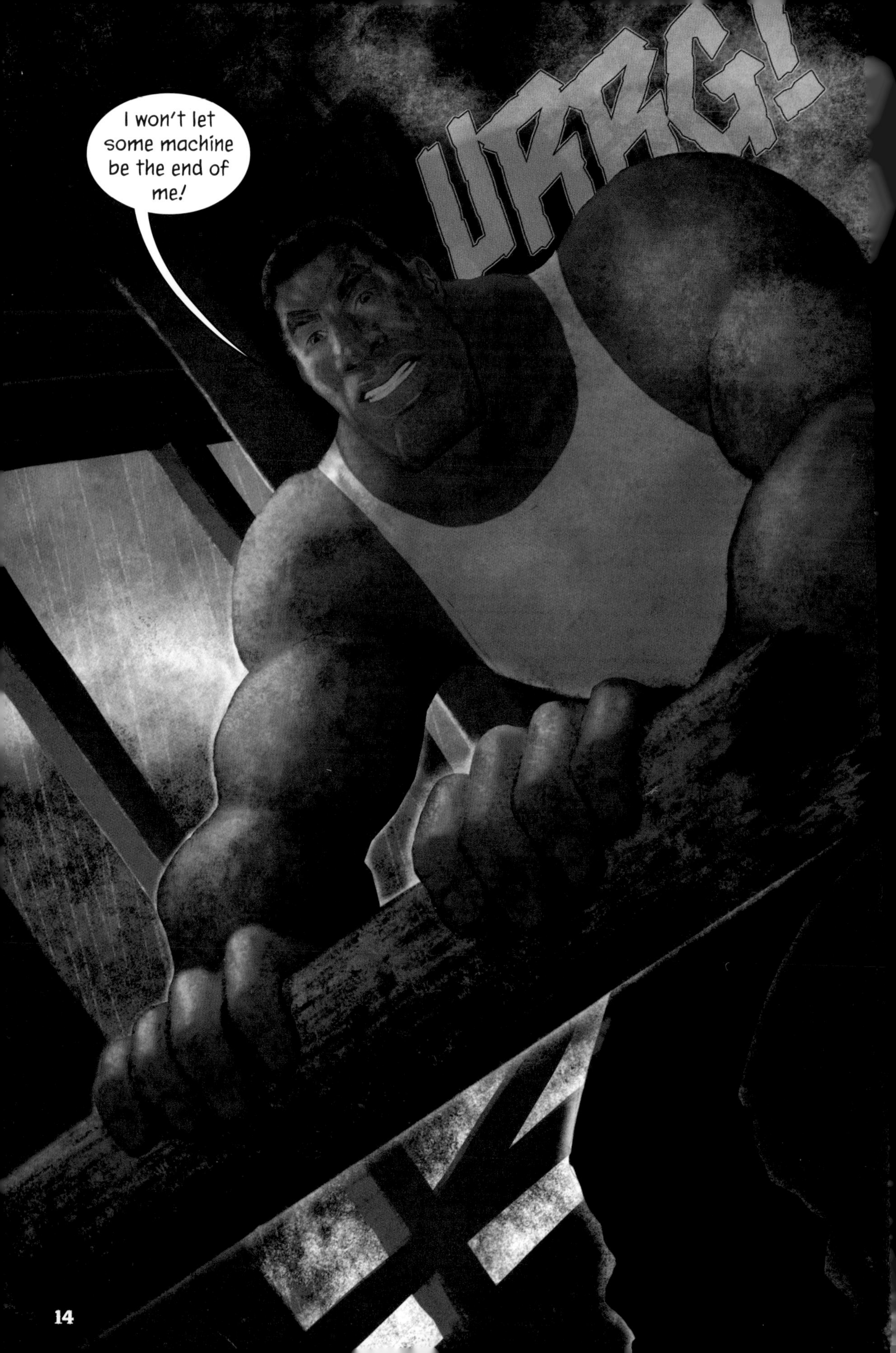
I won't let some machine be the end of me!
URRG!

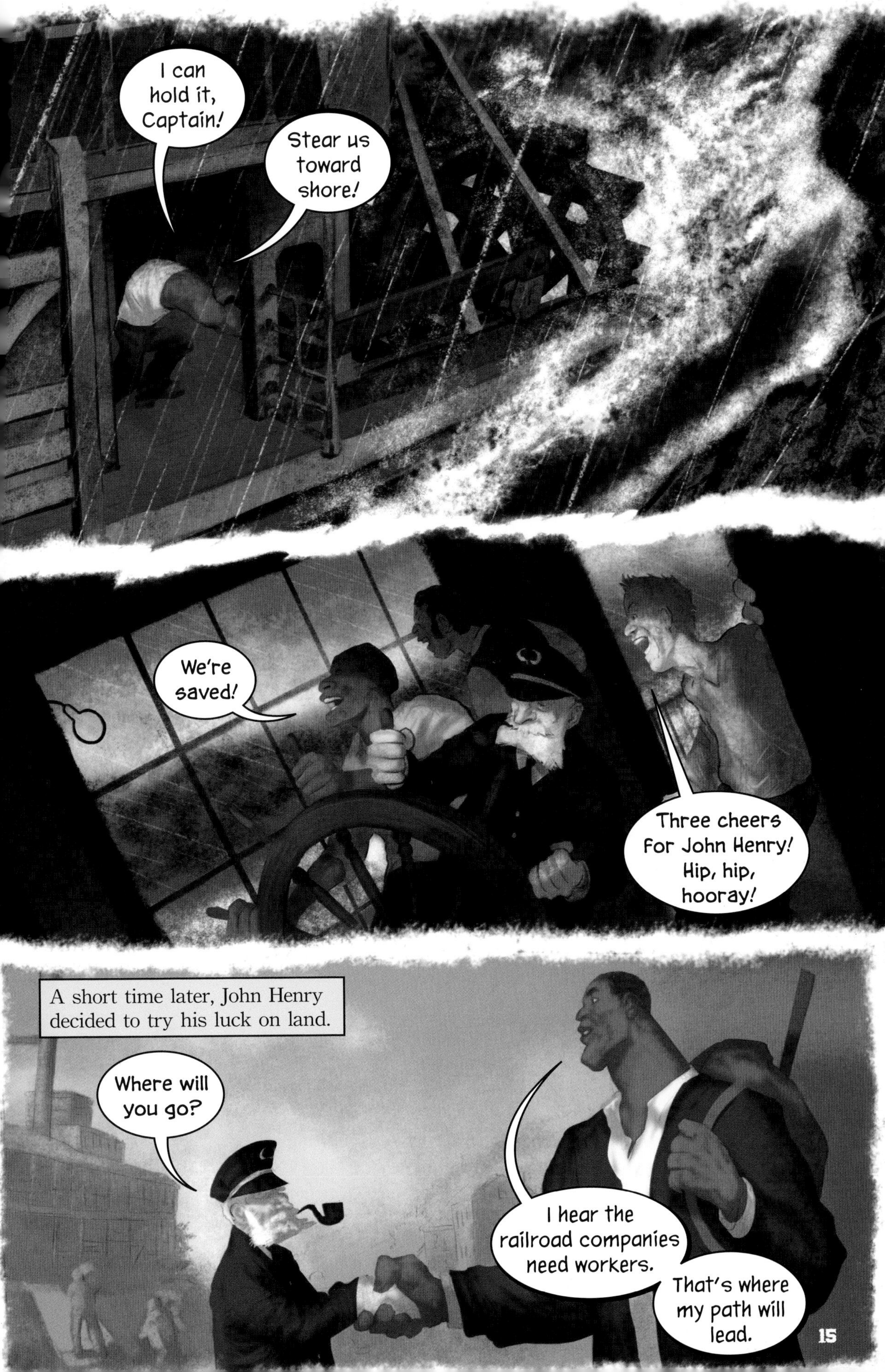
I can hold it, Captain!
Stear us toward shore!
We're saved!
Three cheers for John Henry! Hip, hip, hooray!
A short time later, John Henry decided to try his luck on land.
Where will you go?
I hear the railroad companies need workers.
That's where my path will lead.

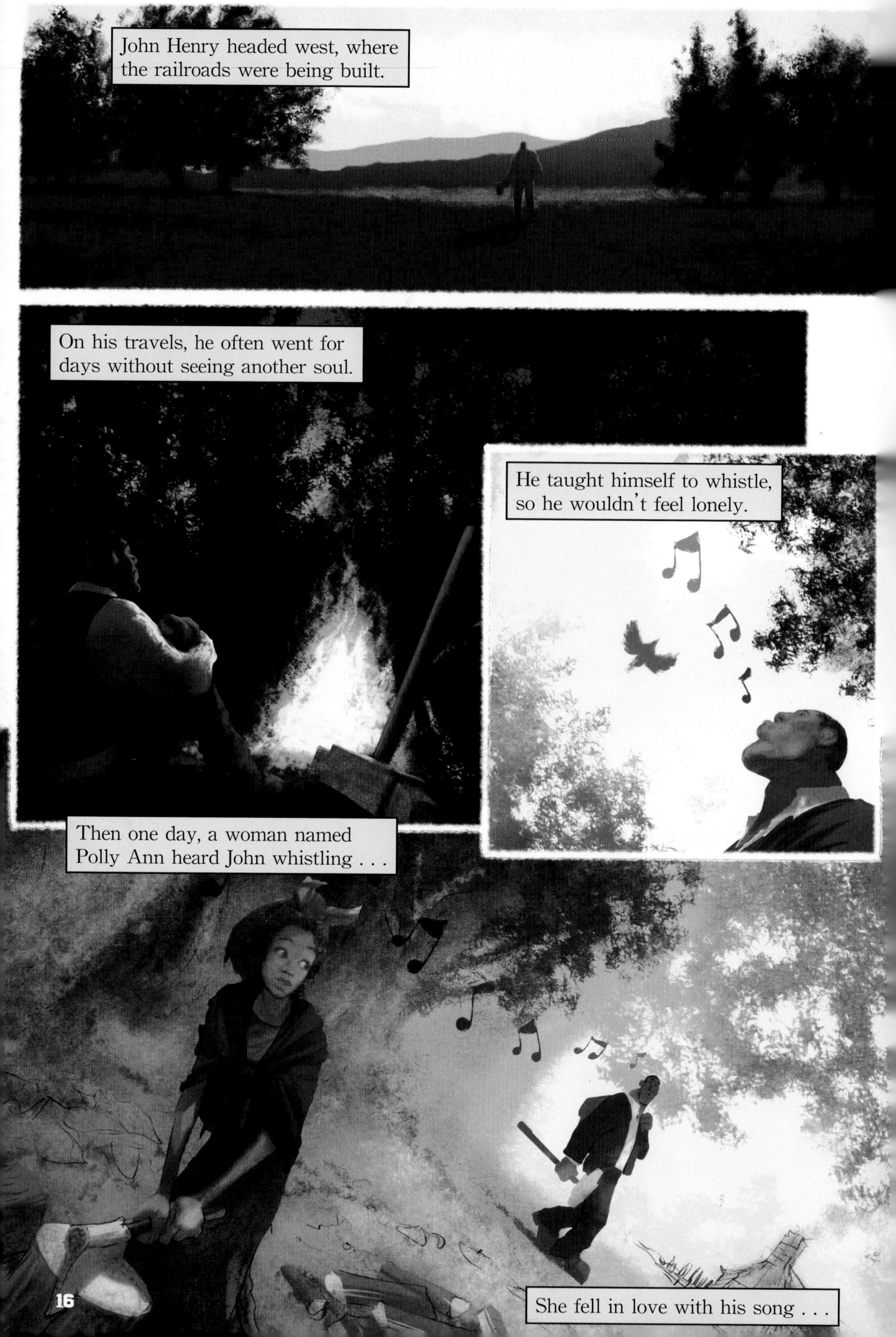
John Henry headed west, where the railroads were being built.
On his travels, he often went for days without seeing another soul.
He taught himself to whistle, so he wouldn't feel lonely.
Then one day, a woman named Polly Ann heard John whistling . . .
She fell in love with his song . . .

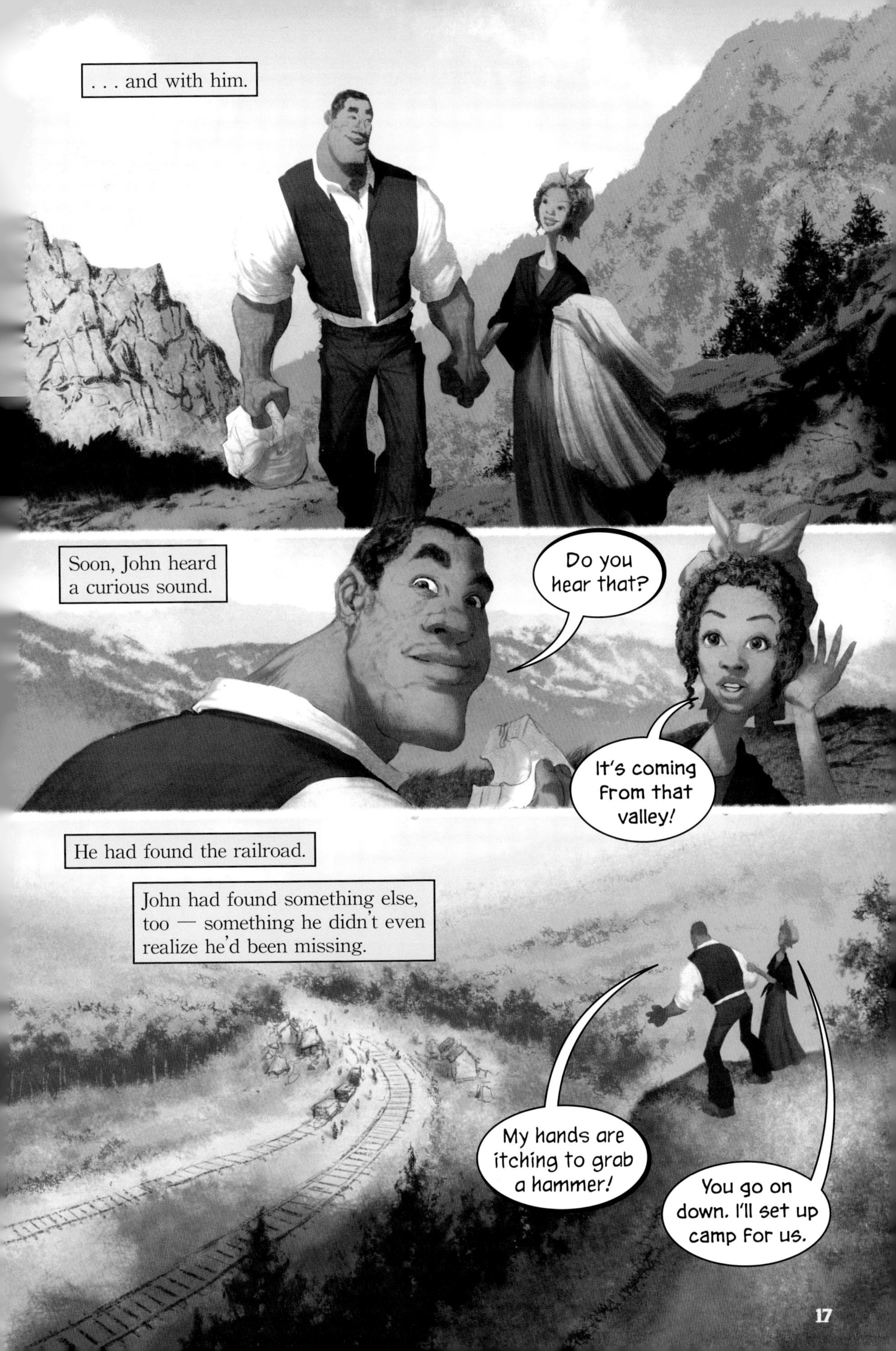
. . . and with him.
Soon, John heard a curious sound.
Do you hear that?
It's coming from that valley!
He had found the railroad.
John had found something else, too — something he didn't even realize he'd been missing.
My hands are itching to grab a hammer!
You go on down. I'll set up camp for us.

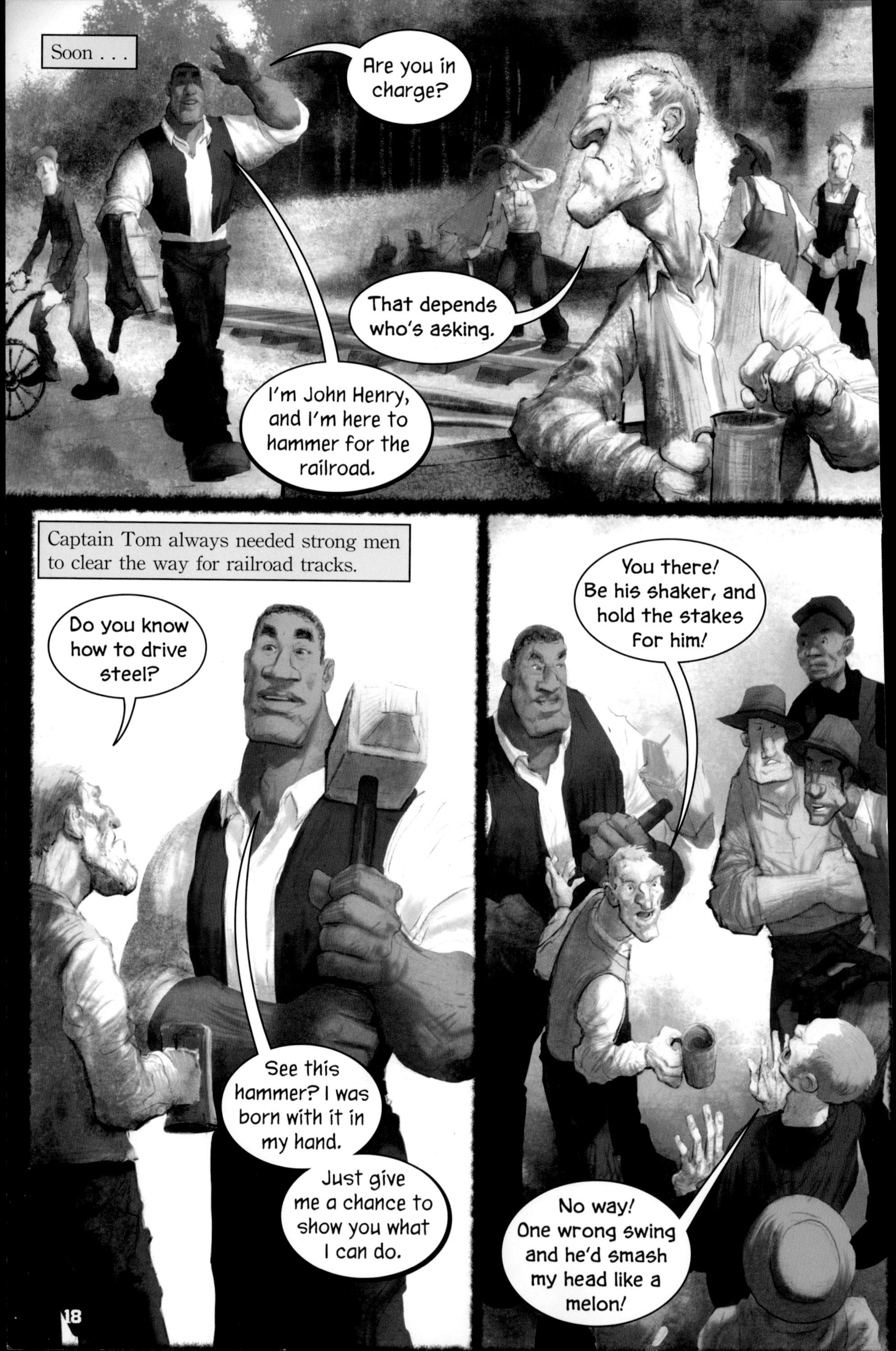
Soon . . .
Are you in charge?
That depends who's asking.
I'm John Henry, and I'm here to hammer for the railroad.
Captain Tom always needed strong men to clear the way for railroad tracks.
Do you know how to drive steel?
See this hammer? I was born with it in my hand.
Just give me a chance to show you what I can do.
You there! Be his shaker, and hold the stakes for him!
No way! One wrong swing and he'd smash my head like a melon!

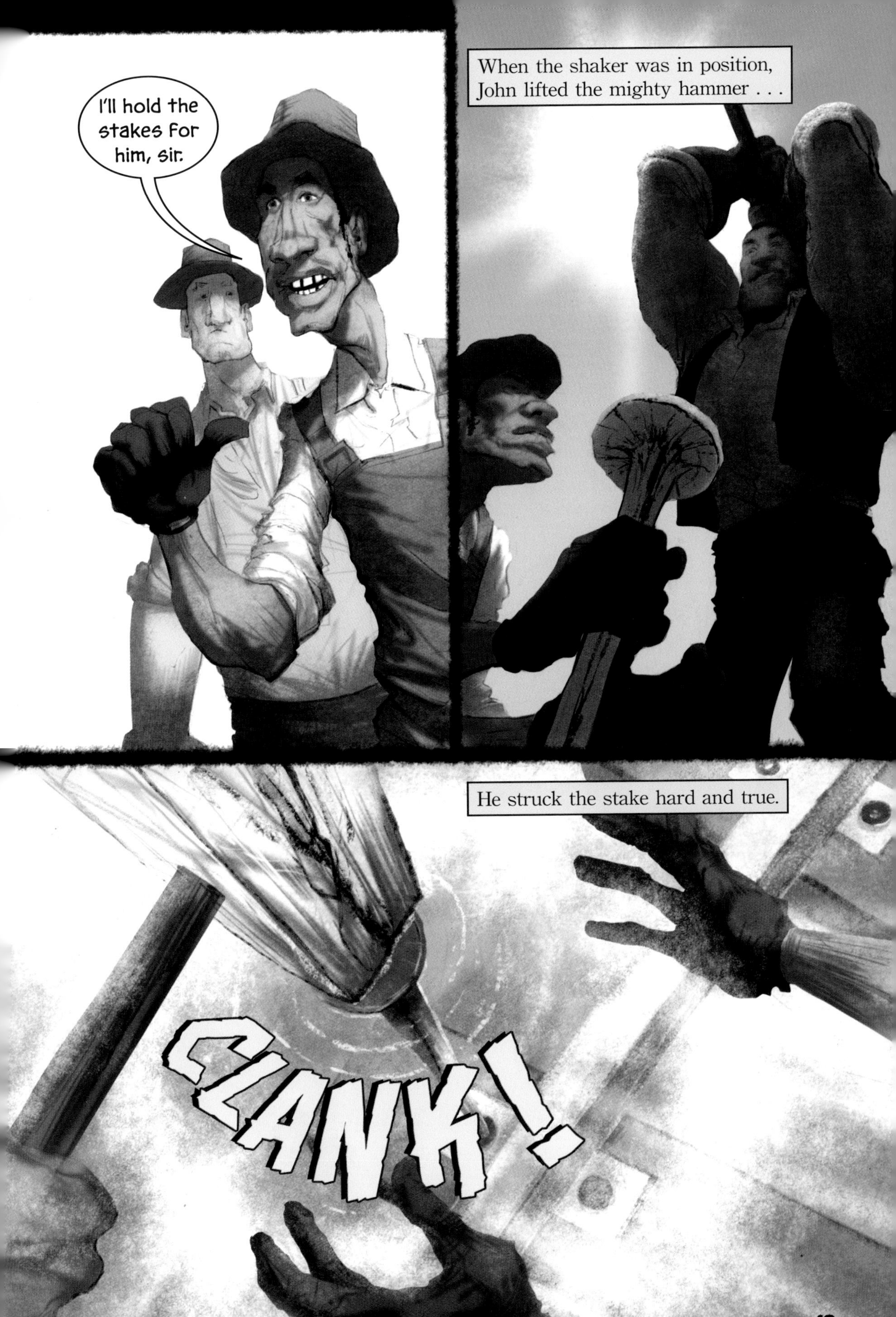
I'll hold the stakes for him, sir.
When the shaker was in position, John lifted the mighty hammer . . .
He struck the stake hard and true.
CLANK!

You're hired!
?
!
!
I've never seen anyone bury a stake with just one swing!

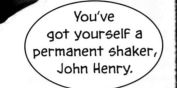

You've got yourself a permanent shaker, John Henry.

PAT
PAT

I'll need a new hammer. Make it two.

And they'll need to be as strong as I am to get this job done right.

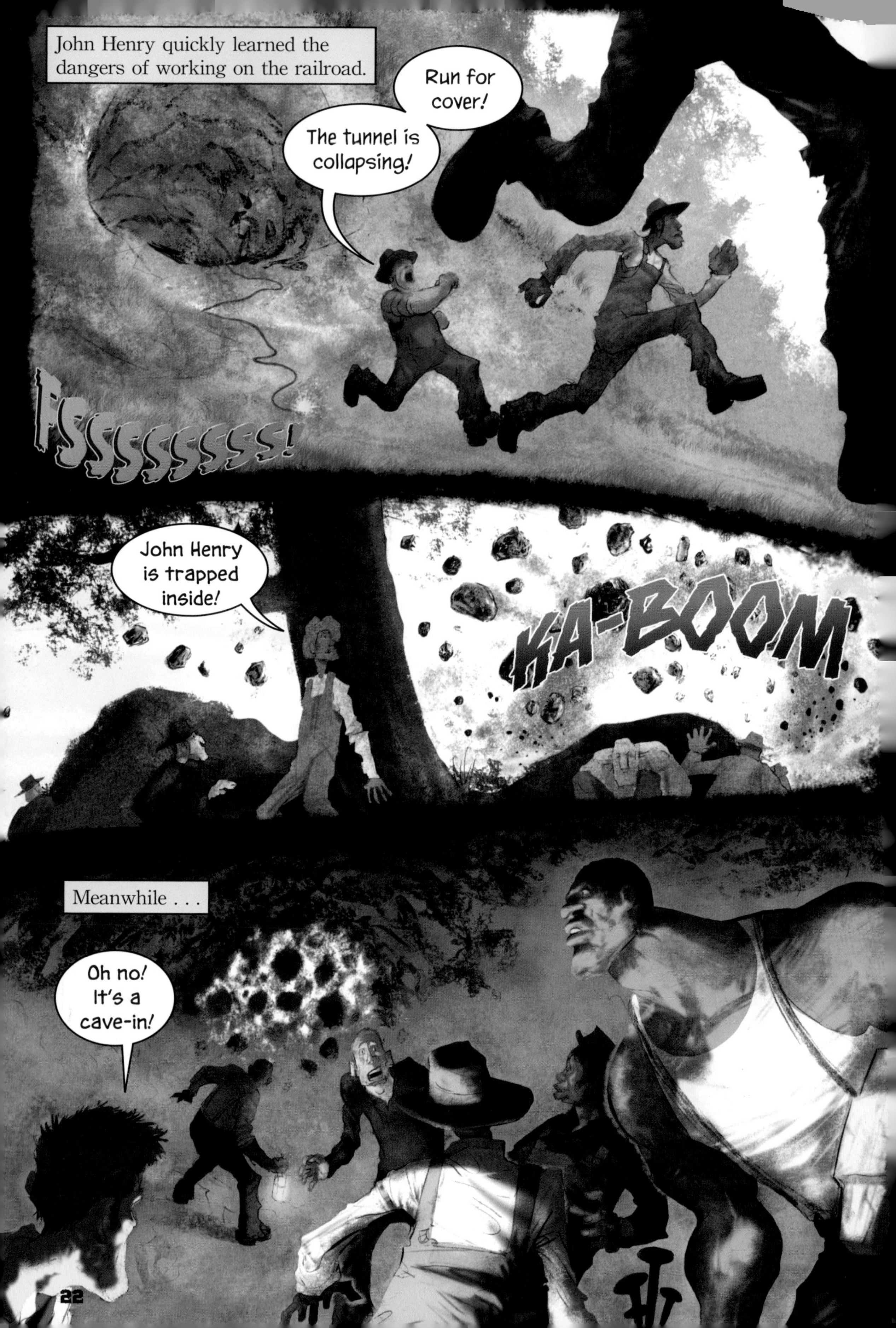
John Henry quickly learned the dangers of working on the railroad.
Run for cover!
The tunnel is collapsing!
FSSSSSSSS!
John Henry is trapped inside!
KA-BOOM
Meanwhile . . .
Oh no! It's a cave-in!

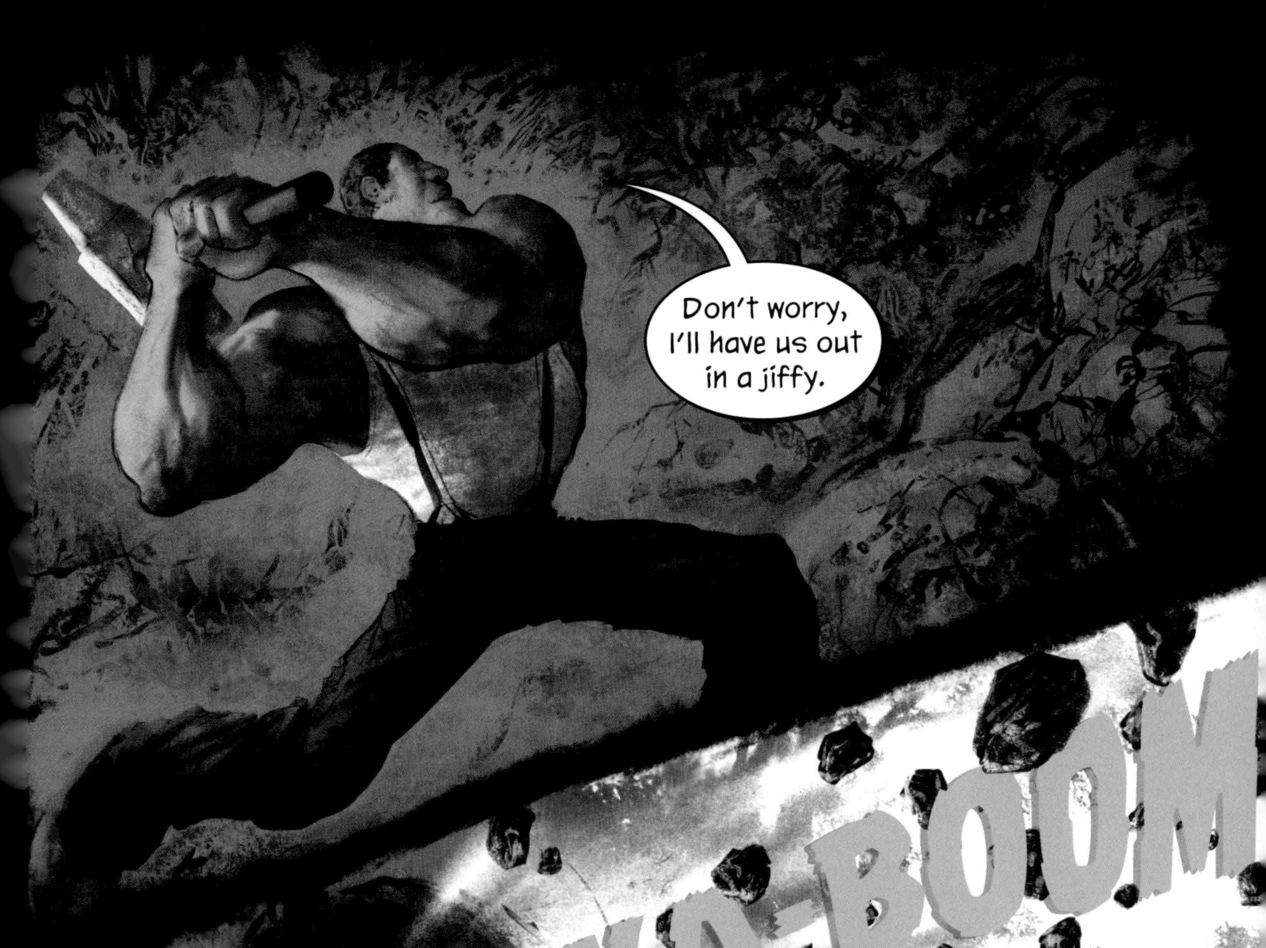
Don't worry, I'll have us out in a jiffy.
KA-BOOM
John Henry's heroic feats soon spread across the railroad lines like a locomotive.

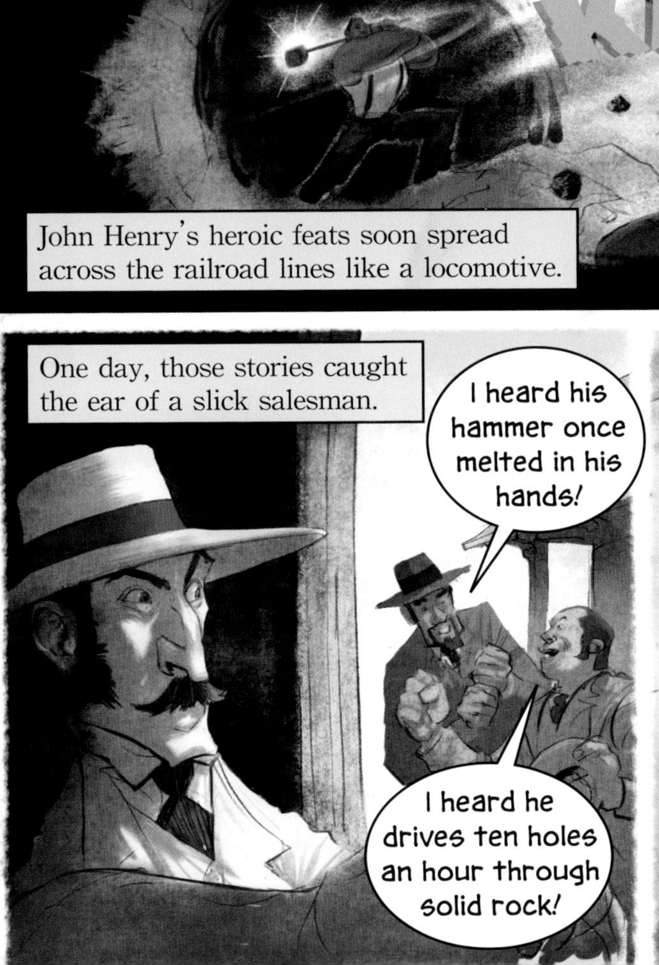
One day, those stories caught the ear of a slick salesman.
I heard his hammer once melted in his hands!
I heard he drives ten holes an hour through solid rock!

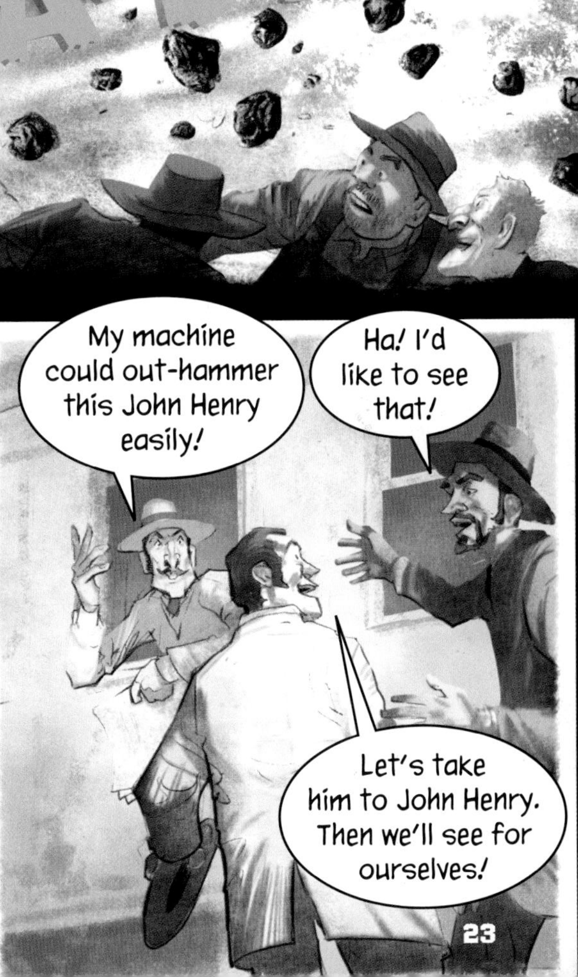
My machine could out-hammer this John Henry easily!
Ha! I'd like to see that!
Let's take him to John Henry. Then we'll see for ourselves!

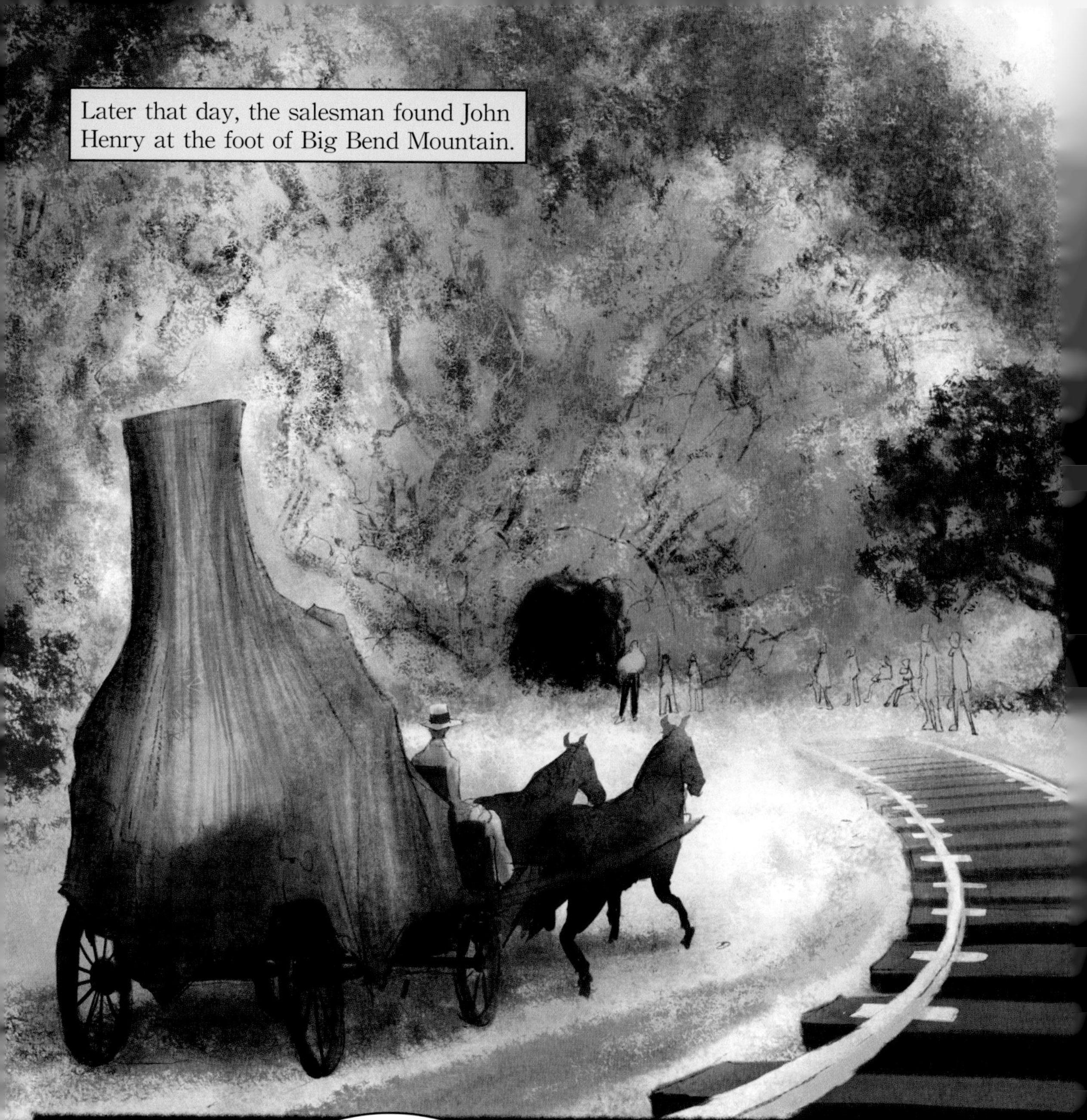

Later that day, the salesman found John Henry at the foot of Big Bend Mountain.

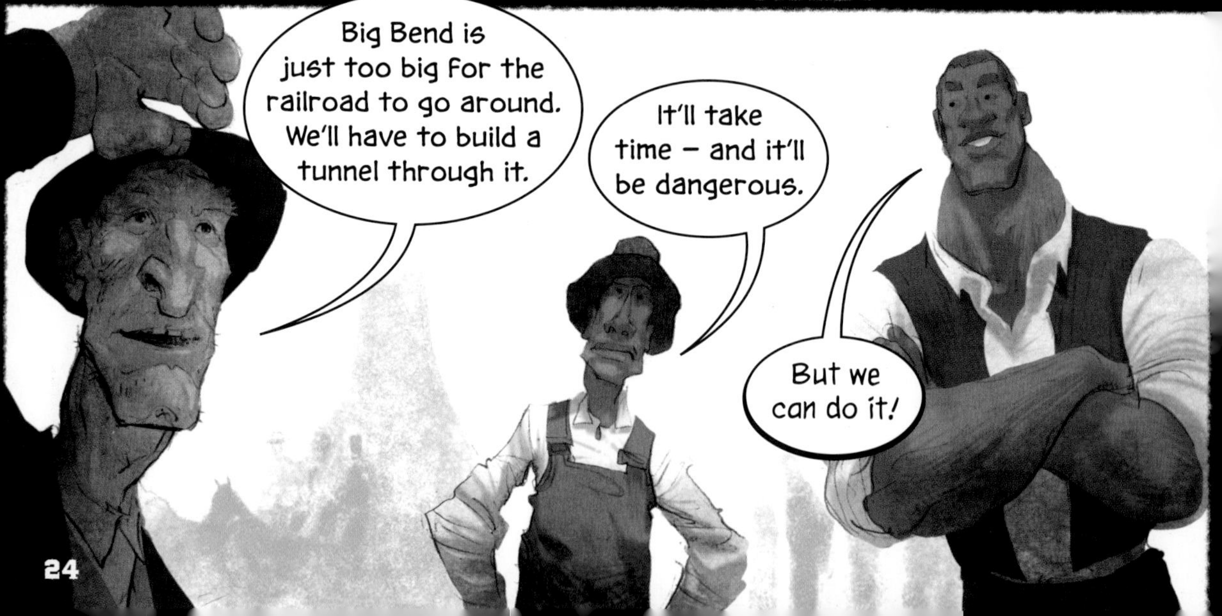

Big Bend is just too big for the railroad to go around. We'll have to build a tunnel through it.
It'll take time — and it'll be dangerous.
But we can do it!

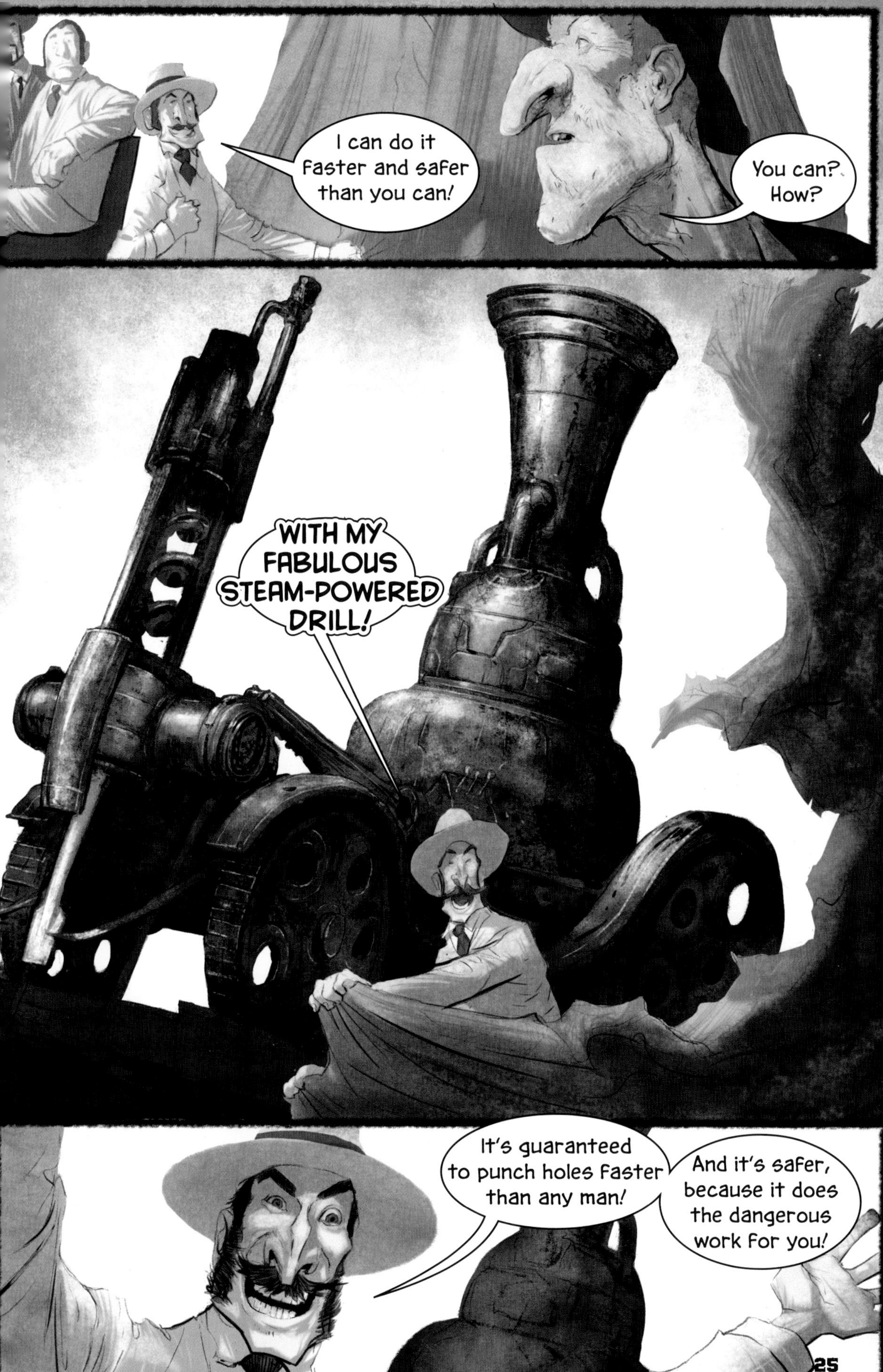

I can do it faster and safer than you can!
You can? How?
WITH MY FABULOUS STEAM-POWERED DRILL!
It's guaranteed to punch holes faster than any man!
And it's safer, because it does the dangerous work for you!

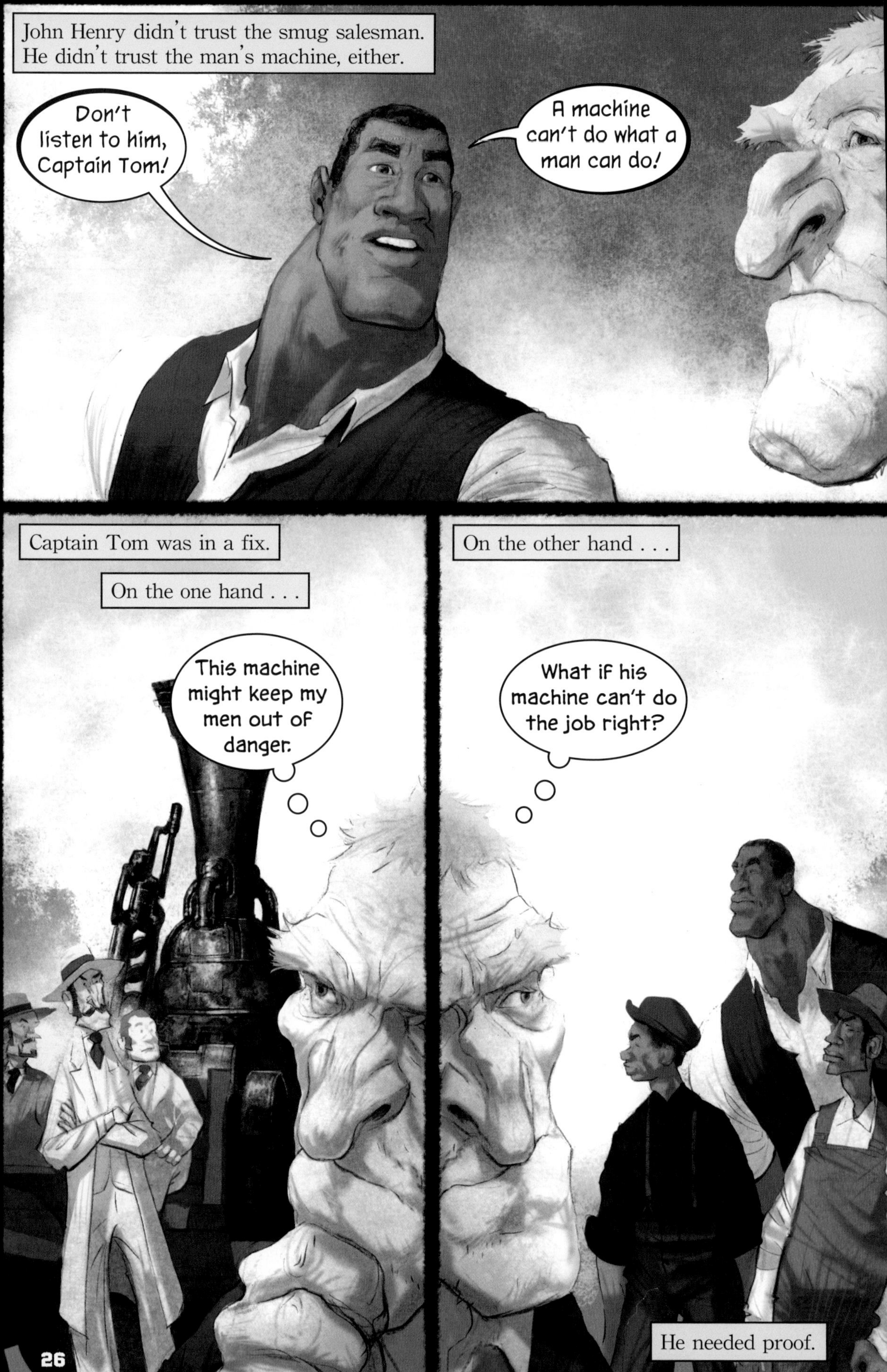
John Henry didn't trust the smug salesman. He didn't trust the man's machine, either.
Don't listen to him, Captain Tom!
A machine can't do what a man can do!
Captain Tom was in a fix.
On the one hand . . .
This machine might keep my men out of danger.
On the other hand . . .
What if his machine can't do the job right?
He needed proof.

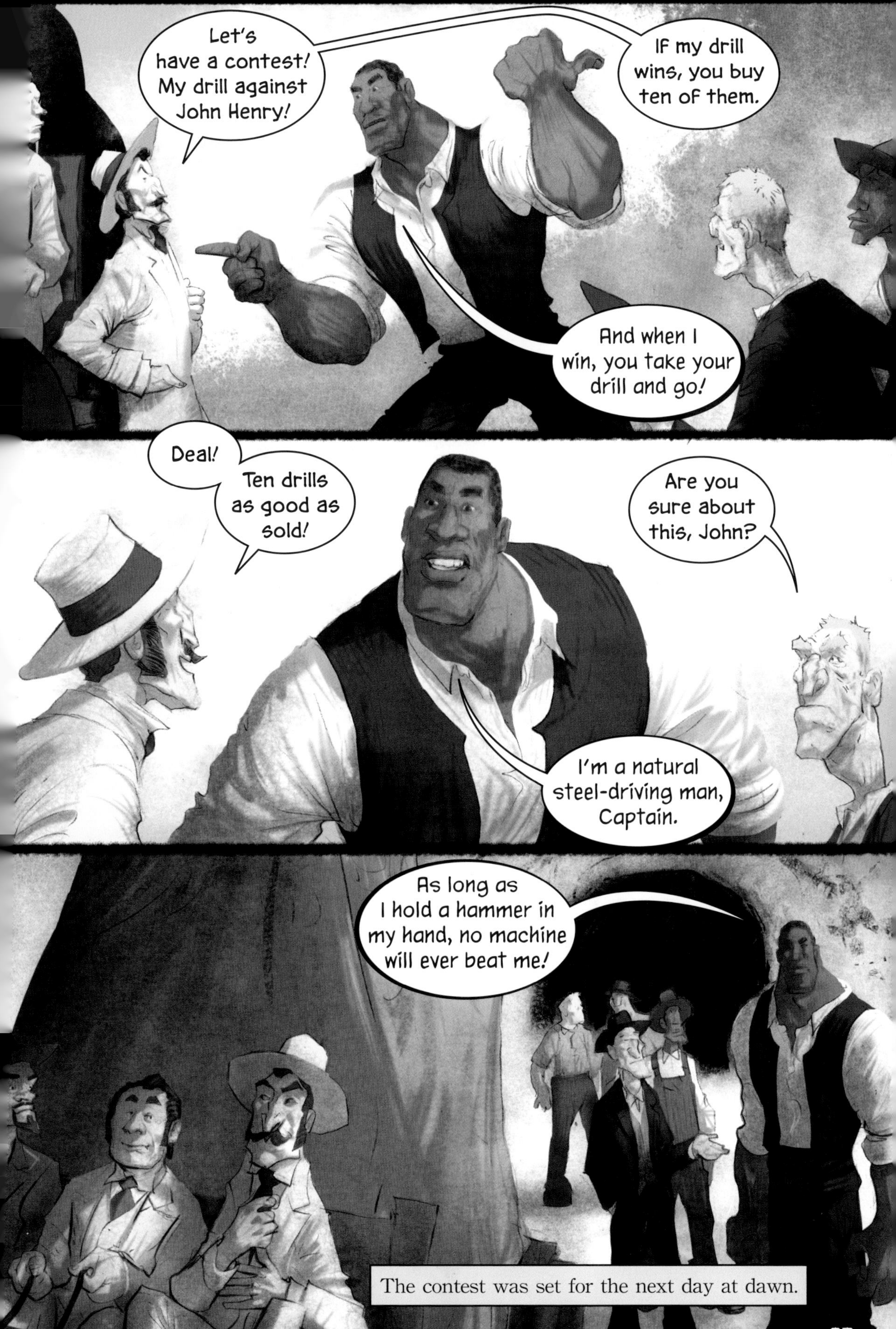
Let's have a contest! My drill against John Henry!
If my drill wins, you buy ten of them.
And when I win, you take your drill and go!
Deal!
Ten drills as good as sold!
Are you sure about this, John?
I'm a natural steel-driving man, Captain.
As long as I hold a hammer in my hand, no machine will ever beat me!
The contest was set for the next day at dawn.

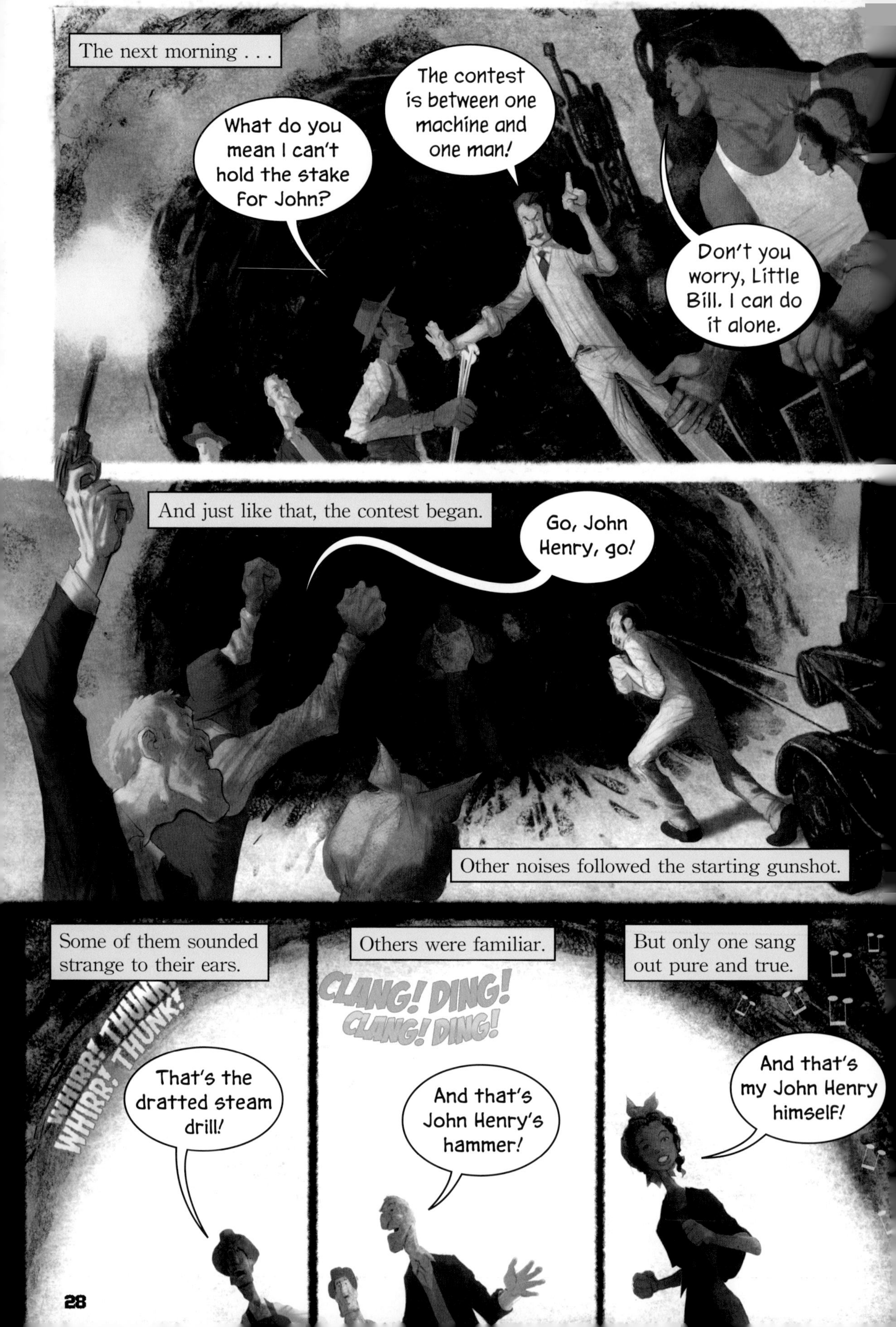
The next morning . . .
What do you mean I can't hold the stake for John?
The contest is between one machine and one man!
Don't you worry, Little Bill. I can do it alone.
And just like that, the contest began.
Go, John Henry, go!
Other noises followed the starting gunshot.
Some of them sounded strange to their ears.
WHIRR! THUNK! WHIRR! THUNK!
That's the dratted steam drill!
Others were familiar.
CLANG! DING! CLANG! DING!
And that's John Henry's hammer!
But only one sang out pure and true.
And that's my John Henry himself!

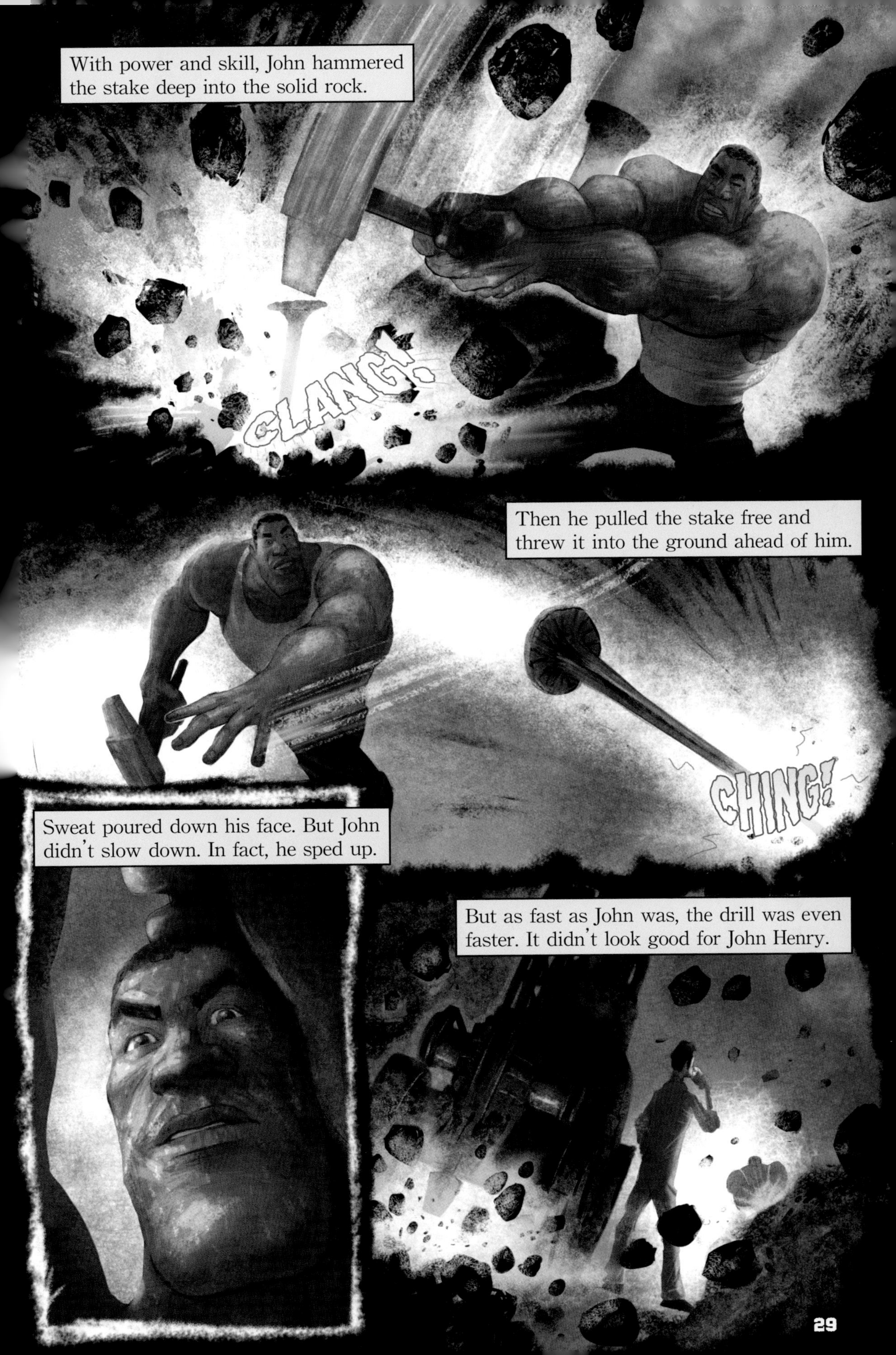
With power and skill, John hammered the stake deep into the solid rock.
CLANG!
Then he pulled the stake free and threw it into the ground ahead of him.
CHING!
Sweat poured down his face. But John didn't slow down. In fact, he sped up.
But as fast as John was, the drill was even faster. It didn't look good for John Henry.

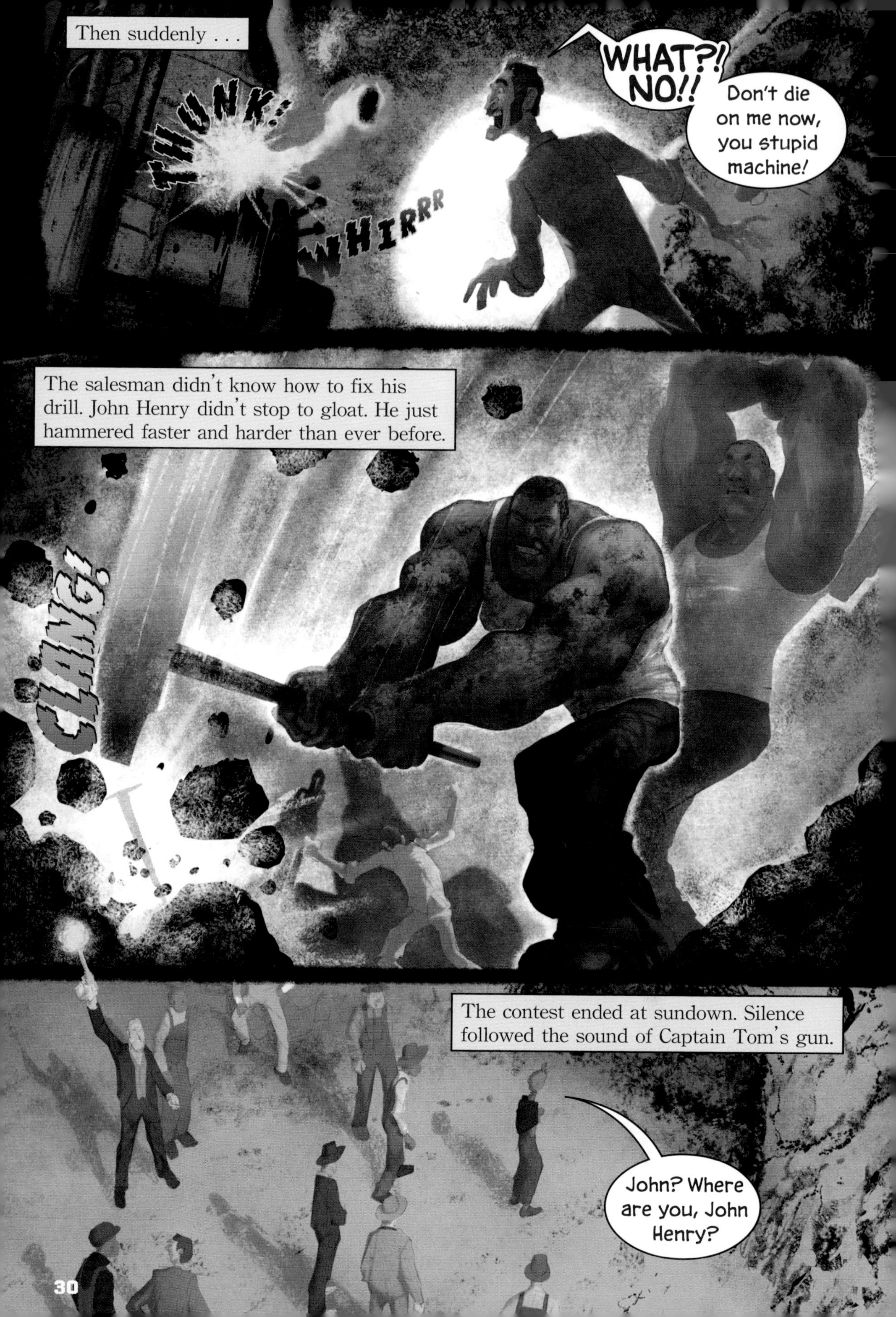

Then suddenly . . .
THUNK!
WHIRRR
WHAT?! NO!!
Don't die on me now, you stupid machine!
The salesman didn't know how to fix his drill. John Henry didn't stop to gloat. He just hammered faster and harder than ever before.
CLANG!
The contest ended at sundown. Silence followed the sound of Captain Tom's gun.
John? Where are you, John Henry?

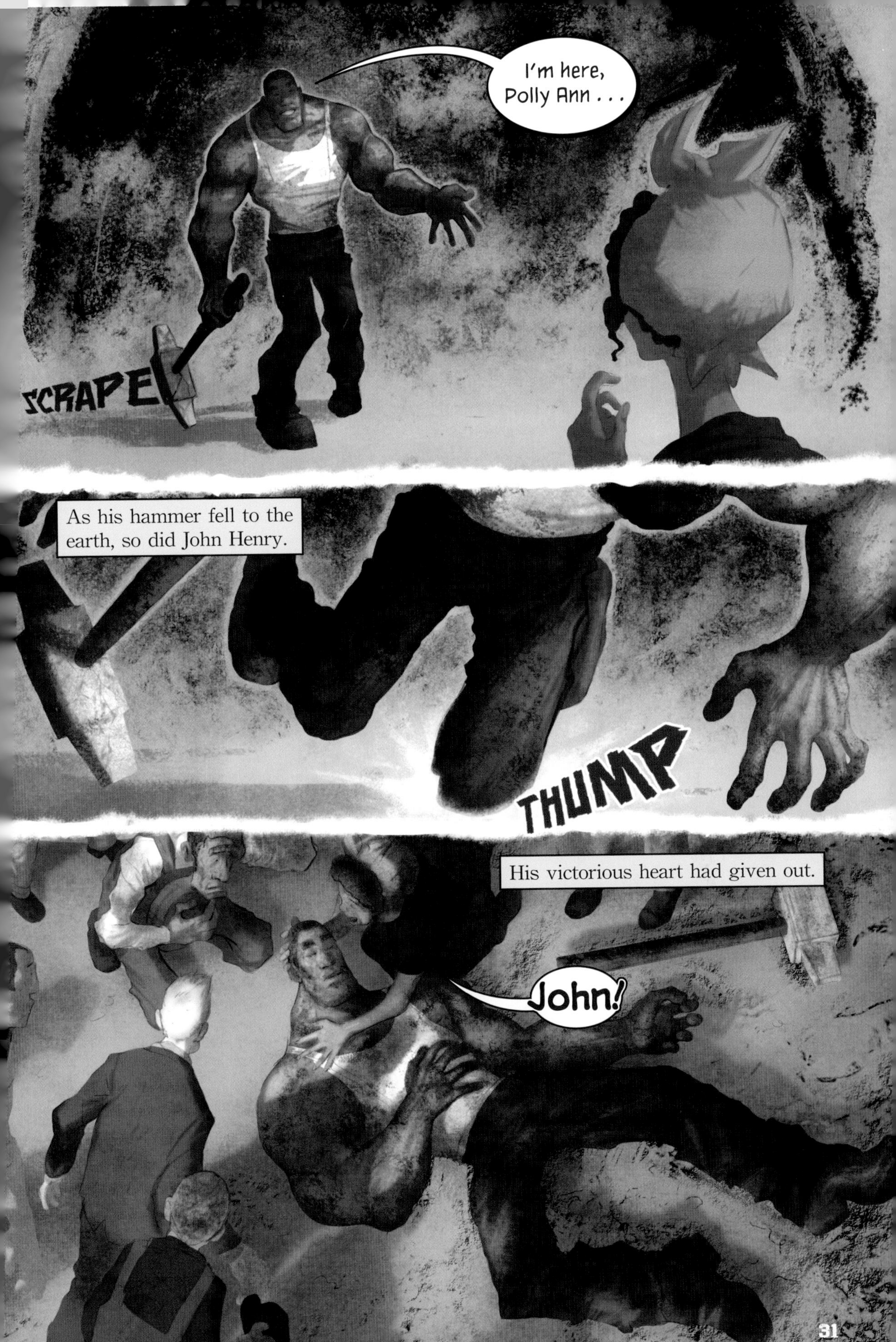
I'm here, Polly Ann . . .
SCRAPE
As his hammer fell to the earth, so did John Henry.
THUMP
His victorious heart had given out.
John!

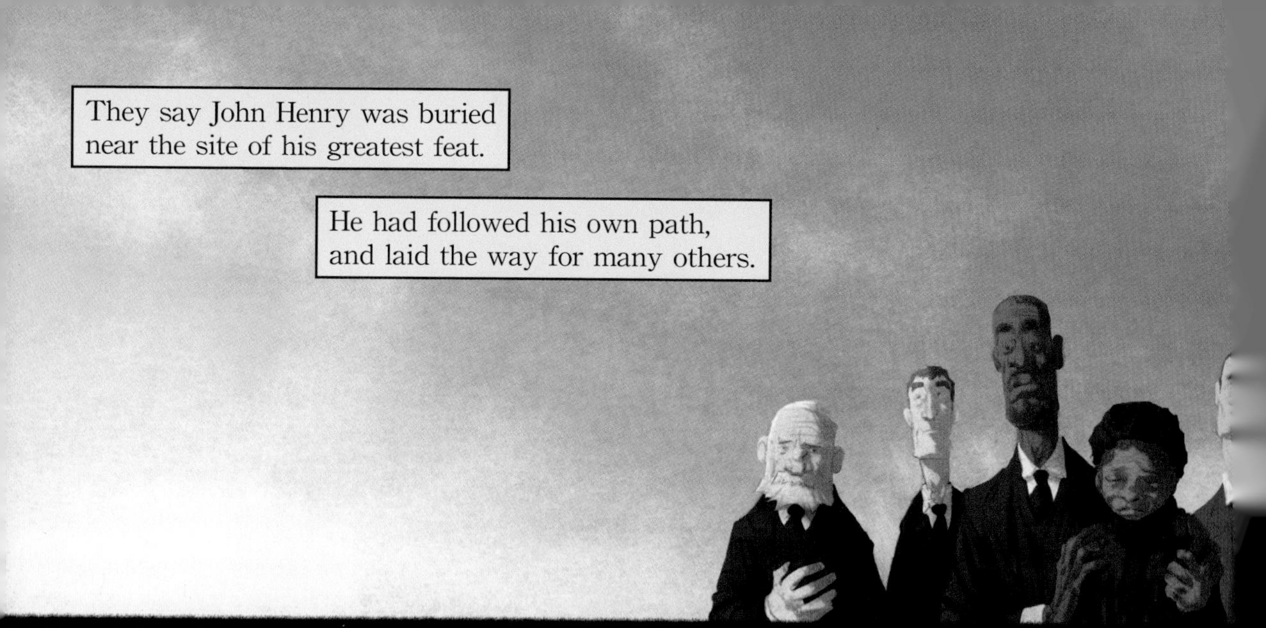
They say John Henry was buried near the site of his greatest feat.
He had followed his own path, and laid the way for many others.

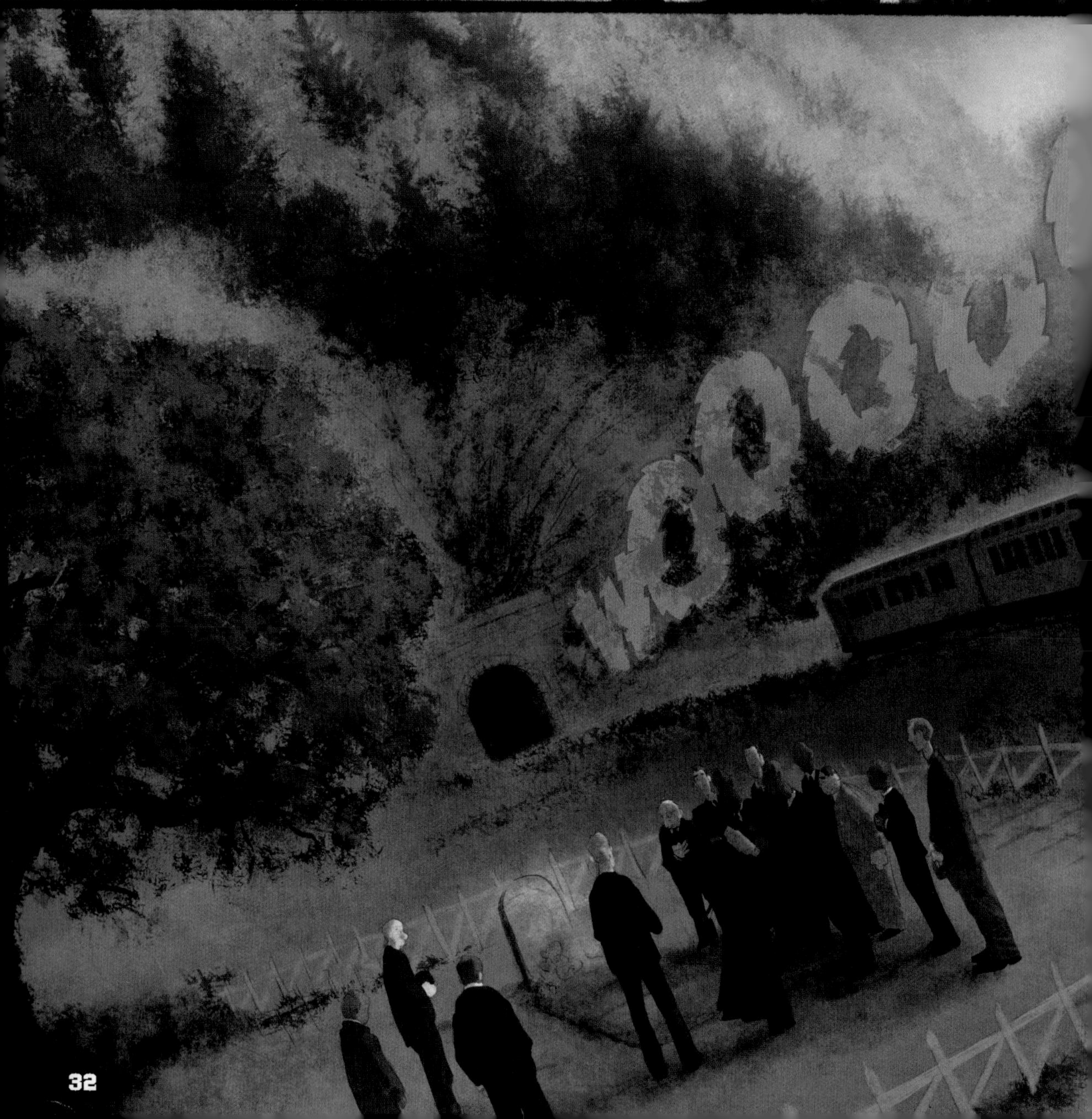
WOOOO

He was a natural, steel-driving man.
His muscles were as strong as iron . . .
. . . And his heart was pure as gold.

THE AUTHOR

Stephanie True Peters started writing books herself after working more than 10 years as a children's book editor. She has since written 40 books, including the New York Times best seller A Princess Primer: A Fairy Godmother's Guide to Being a Princess. When not at her computer, Peters enjoys playing with her two children, hitting the gym, or working on home improvement projects with her patient and supportive husband, Daniel.

THE ILLUSTRATOR

Nelson Evergreen lives on the south coast of the United Kingdom with his partner and their imaginary cat. Evergreen is a comic artist, illustrator, and general all-around doodler of whatever nonsense pops into his head. He contributes regularly to the British underground comics scene, and is currently writing and illustrating a number of graphic novel and picture book hybrids for older children.

GLOSSARY

appetite (AP-uh-tite)—desire for food, or a great enjoyment of something

feat (FEET)—an achievement that shows great courage, strength, or skill

guarantee (ga-ruhn-TEE)—a promise that something will definitely happen

locomotive (loh-kuh-MOH-tiv)—an engine used to push or pull railroad cars

pistons (PISS-tuhnz)—disks or cylinders that push back and forth in a large cylinder. Their back and forth motion is converted to rotational motion, which creates movement in an engine.

shaker (SHAY-kur)—a railroad worker who holds the stakes steady while another railroad worker hammers them in

steam powered (STEEM POW-urd)—something that's powered by steam. As water boils, it creates steam. This steam is forced into cylinders where it pushes pistons to operate machinery.

steel (STEEL)—a hard, strong metal made mostly from iron

trusty (TRUHSS-tee)—reliable, dependable, or capable of being trusted

victorious (vik-TAWR-ee-uhss)—if something or someone is victorious, it has won a battle or a contest

TAKE A TRIP
BACK IN TIME ON THE...

JOHN HENRY RAILROAD TOUR

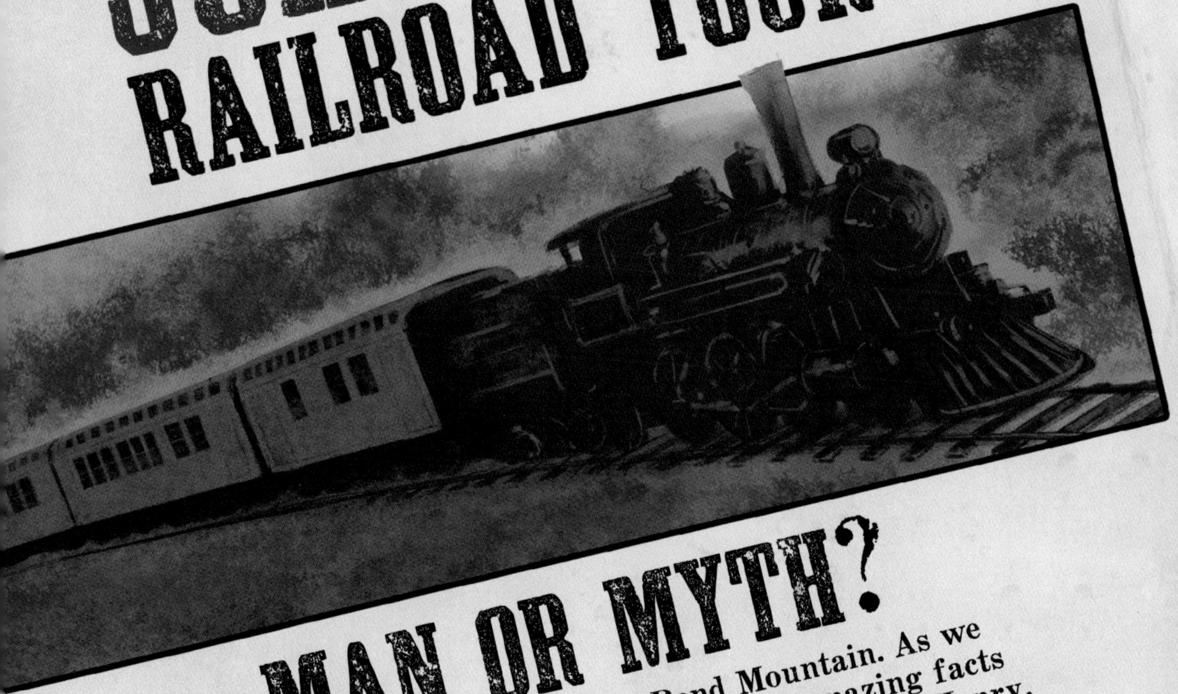

MAN OR MYTH?

We begin our journey along Big Bend Mountain. As we travel, we'll share some of the history and amazing facts behind the stories of the steel-driving legend, John Henry.

MEET THE MAN

History says that John Henry likely drove steel here in the Great Bend Tunnel in the early 1870s. Records state there was a man of that name working then for the C & O railroad company. Witnesses say that he competed against a steam drill and beat it, too. It is less likely, however, that John died from over-exertion after the contest, although several historians think that John Henry died shortly after his triumph against the machine.

LEARN THE LEGEND

Legend states that John Henry was a slave in the 1840s and 1850s. Once freed, he set out to make his mark on the world, and eventually did so on the great American railroads. They say he was six feet tall and weighed 200 pounds — impressively large for people of that time. Many more tales were told of his beautiful baritone singing voice, his enormous appetite, and his renowned whistling and banjo-playing abilities.

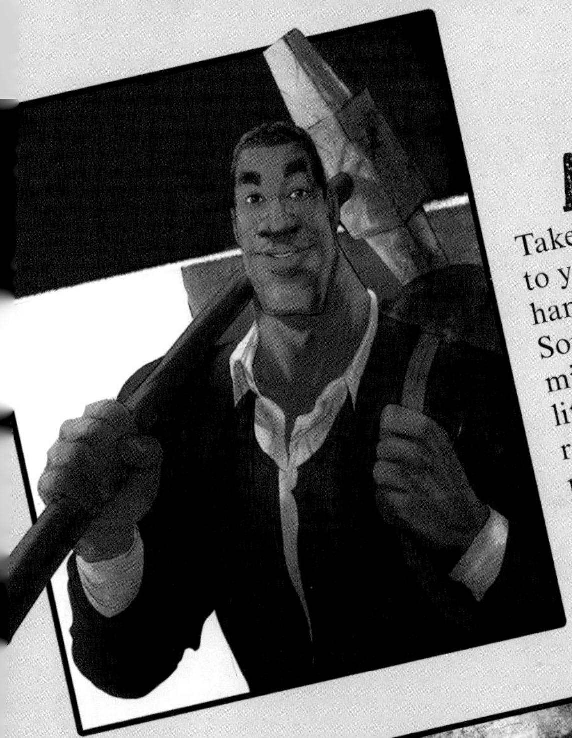

AMAZING ARTIFACTS

Take a peak at the huge hammer of John Henry to your left! Railroad men in John's time used hammers that weighed as much as nine pounds. Some days, the railroad workers laid more than a mile of track per day in the sweltering heat with little water or food. Steel drivers drove holes into rock with steel drills or spikes. A hammer man's partner, known as a shaker, kneeled close to the hole and rotated the drill after each strike of the hammer.

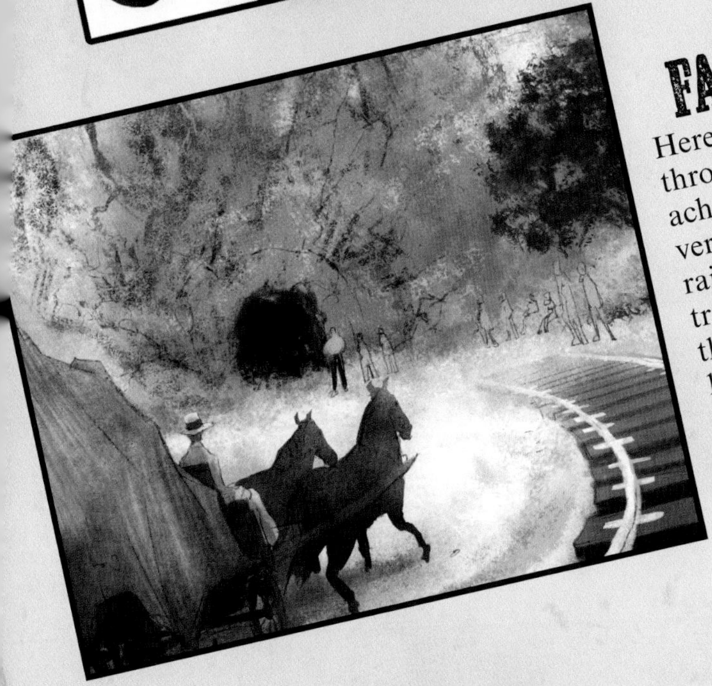

FANTASTIC FEATS

Here in Big Bend Tunnel, we travel through one of John's greatest achievements — his work on this very passageway. John and his fellow railroad men blasted holes and laid track for more than a mile directly through Big Bend Mountain. It took 1,000 men three years to complete this impressive tunnel.

PLACES TO SEE

Turn your eyes upward and you'll see Big Bend Mountain, the famous site of John Henry's epic battle between man and machine. Look to the right, above the Big Bend Tunnel, and you will see the eight-foot tall, bronze statue of John Henry here in Talcott, West Virginia, in all of its full-sized splendor.

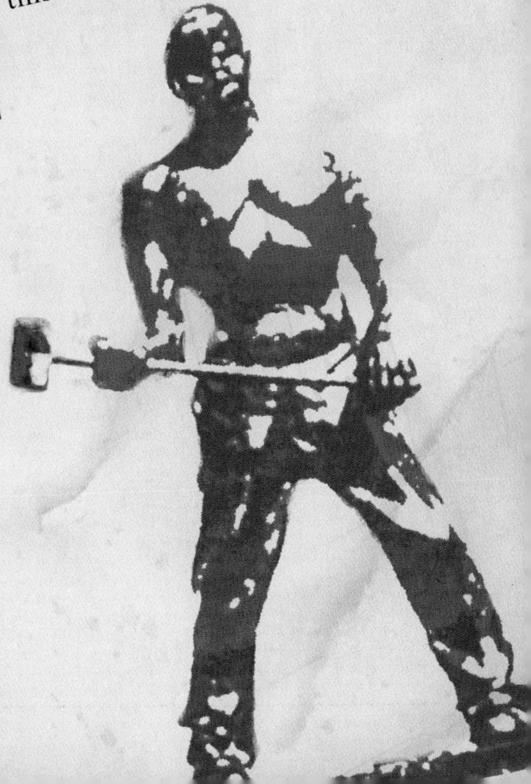

DISCUSSION QUESTIONS

1. In this book, John Henry says that human labor is better than work done by machines. What are the advantages and disadvantages of both kinds of labor?

2. Each page of this book has several illustrations, called panels. Which panel in this book is your favorite? Why?

3. In your opinion, what made John Henry a hero? Discuss your answers.

WRITING PROMPTS

1. After John Henry becomes a free man, he starts to look for a job. What kind of work do you want to do when you graduate? Where do you want to live? Write about your future.

2. Tall tales usually involve lots of exaggeration. Which parts of this book could have been real, and which parts seem to be made up? Write about your opinion of this tall tale.

3. When he was growing up, John Henry's favorite toy was his hammer. When you were a kid, what was your favorite toy? What kinds of things did you do for fun? Write about your childhood.

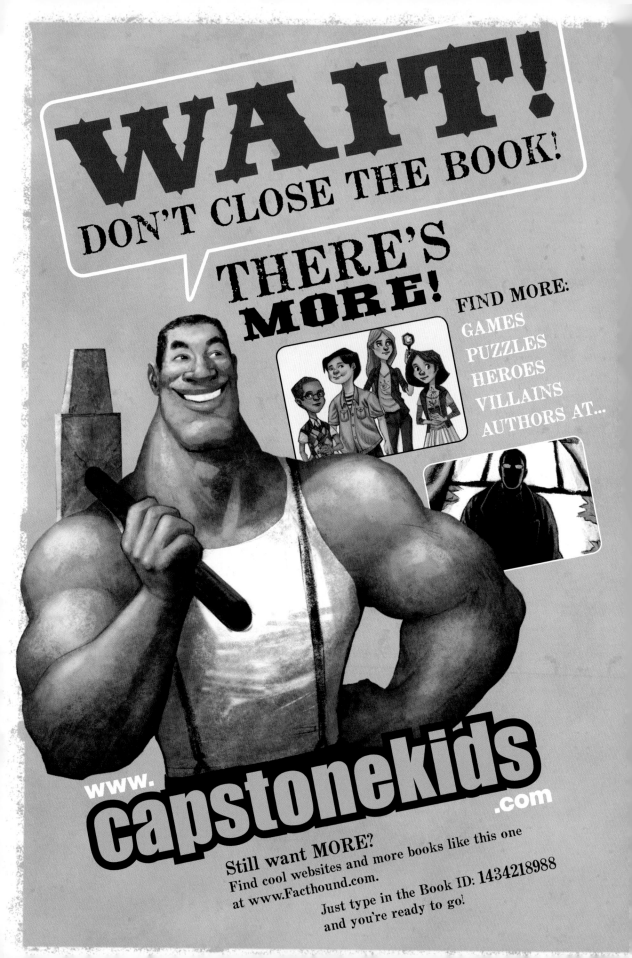